My attention was diverted. In the shadowy corner of the room, *she'd* moved. The being—person—entity—I called "my specter". She stared at me, her face expressionless, featureless. Just those black hollow eyes. I could see the far wall through her, its soft gray misted by her white silhouette. She opened her impression of a mouth. No lips, no tongue or teeth visible. Just a round black hole, which opened in her face and formed a triangle with her eyes. She always tried to speak. But no words ever came, just waves of loneliness—fear even—and a sense that her real purpose had yet to be fulfilled. Yet, whenever I thought that, a nameless and overpowering dread enveloped me.

SAVING GRACE DEVINE

CATHERINE CAVENDISH

Dedication

To Colin, without whom…

Acknowledgments

A massive thank you to my friend and fellow horror author, Steve Emmett, who patiently read through an early draft, pointed out the errors of my ways and gave me a swift kick where necessary. Another big thank you to my horror writer friend, Julia Kavan, for all her wisdom, friendship and sage advice. Thanks also to historical fiction writer, Shehanne Moore for her friendship and support.

Huge thanks to Don D'Auria, and to all at Crossroad Press.

J ust one more step…

I look down. It would be so easy. One step. An instant's pain and then…oblivion.

I look to the left, at a platform full of commuters. Monday rush hour. All plugged in to iPods or chatting in broken sentences on their phones.

A swift glance to the right. A girl with impossibly black hair and multi-colored nails, lurid with Technicolor swirls. Her phone conversation is the most important thing in the world to her.

"Oh my God, Stacey. No…he was like…yes…and I was like…you know."

Every phrase is punctuated by her free hand, touching her face, clenching and unclenching or covering her mouth to emphasize her amazement.

No, she wouldn't notice, would she?

I glance up at the display. 'HERE' is flashing. The train approaches. I hear the iron rails clang and switch my attention to the left again. I see its lights as it veers around the curve.

"OMG, Stacey, that's *sick!*"

And I know she means it's the best thing she's heard in days. My left foot trembles as it hovers over the edge.

A stray tear tracks its lonely and unloved way down my cheek.

Now…Now…

The passengers mill in anticipation, jockeying for position. Some end phone conversations. The train's almost here. Soon it will be traveling too slowly.

Now…or never…
I take another step forward.

Chapter One

"You can look at this one of two ways, Alex. Either as a threat or an opportunity. If I were you, I know which I'd choose."

I accepted the glass of Merlot Greg thrust at me and looked up at him. Ten years we'd been married and in all that time he'd never steered me wrong. Same with his clients, I suppose. One glance at those blue eyes and his self-confidence shot into your veins. Somehow he managed to make you as sure as he was that all would be well.

So why didn't it work for me now? Because today I had been told I was redundant.

Fifteen years of toil for the Central Library only to be tossed aside like one of our old books. No, I definitely hadn't planned it this way. Twenty years ago, an eighteen-year-old girl with bright eyes and a clear head had mapped out her life. A degree in librarianship, steady climb up the career ladder and, along the way, a husband and two kids. Well, I acquired the degree, the career progression, and Greg had come along just at the right time, but the kids didn't emerge. Not that I had ever been the type who would be defined by having children—any more than Greg. We were all prepared for it, of course. Comfortable three-bedroom semi in a respectable middle-class suburb, close to schools with the right reputations, but the years went by and nothing happened. Neither of us worried and neither of us bothered to have ourselves checked out. At thirty-nine, I still didn't feel I'd missed out on anything. But I hadn't planned on losing my job, had I? What would I focus on now?

"You always said you'd write a book when you retire," Greg said.

I managed a wry smile. "I'm a bit too young to retire yet."

He grinned, his teeth white and even against his dark beard. Some men lose themselves behind facial hair but it suited Greg somehow.

"You don't *have* to look for another job yet," he said. "The business is doing well and we've got money in the bank. Tell you what, I'll put you on the books, pay your National Insurance contributions and a small salary. You can work for me."

I laughed. "You know I'm hopeless at figures. I..." My attention was diverted. In the shadowy corner of the room, *she'd* moved. The being—person—entity—I called "my specter". She stared at me, her face expressionless, featureless. Just those black hollow eyes. I could see the far wall through her, its soft gray misted by her white silhouette. She opened her impression of a mouth. No lips, no tongue or teeth visible. Just a round black hole, which opened in her face and formed a triangle with her eyes. She always tried to speak. But no words ever came, just waves of loneliness—fear even—and a sense that her real purpose had yet to be fulfilled. Yet, whenever I thought that, a nameless and overpowering dread enveloped me.

You're a bit late this time. Could she read my mind? I used to think so. At any rate, she *was* late. At least, I thought so at the time. After all, I'd already lost my job. *Where were you yesterday?*

I became aware of Greg speaking. "Are you okay, Alex? You look as white as —oh no, not again. Tell me it's not happening again."

I tore my gaze away from my specter, saw his creased forehead, the downturn of his lips, and braced myself.

"I thought you were done with all that nonsense. You know it's just tricks of the light, shadows moving... Your mind makes up the rest."

I lowered my eyes and nodded. He shook his head and strode over to the drinks cabinet to refill his whisky glass. I stole another look over to where she had stood just moments before. But she'd gone, as I knew she would.

We didn't speak of it again. In fact, Greg spoke barely another word all evening. He settled down to watch a film on TV, which I stared at but didn't take in. Yet another action hero had been transported from the pages of a comic book into a Hollywood blockbuster. Big deal. My thoughts were all on my specter. Trick of the light was she? But tricks of the light don't come dressed in a pale blue gown, white shawl and lace bonnet. Tricks of the light don't stare at you with hollow eyes or beckon to you, or try to speak to you. And they don't come to you in the night and tweak your bedclothes.

Greg would never understand and nor did I, why I could see her and no one else could and why she had attached herself to me. I had no idea who she was, even though she had been a part of my life, on and off, since I was around eleven years old.

Normally her visits presaged some momentous event, such as the night my mother died. My specter appeared, silently weeping, sending out wave after wave of emotional torment that felt strong enough to be physical. Then the police came and told me my mother had been found in her bathroom, with her wrists slashed. No one ever prepares you for such agony. No one ever explains how to get over it. So you don't. Not really.

Some people might have found my specter's appearance frightening. I suppose I did at first—a little anyway. But the night of my mother's suicide, I just wanted her to appear and comfort me, even though she had never shown any ability to do so before.

I hadn't seen my specter for five years or more. The last time was when my father died, officially from a heart attack but, in reality, he had just faded in the three years since my mother took her own life. Death came, for him, as a happy release, and my specter had been less tragic that night.

So, why *had* she come back now?

"Alex?"

I snapped back to reality and met Greg's concerned eyes. He'd switched off the TV and I hadn't even noticed. For some reason I couldn't fathom, a feeling of despair washed over me and I burst into tears.

His arms were around me in an instant and I leaned against his shoulder, burying myself in his warmth. "All right, that's it; we're going away for a couple of weeks. You've had an awful shock and you need time to come to terms with it."

I struggled to catch my breath through my sobs. "But we knew it was in the cards.

We've known for months."

He rocked me gently back and forth, as if soothing a child. "I know, I know, but it's like when you know someone's going to die. You know it's inevitable but it's still a hell of a shock when it happens. And a hell of a wrench too. You've been there so long, and these past weeks, you've had to be strong for your staff. Being a manager's a bitch sometimes."

He handed me a tissue and I blew my nose, turning the soft paper into mulch. He handed me another.

"I know one thing," I said, making a great effort to control myself, "whatever I do in the future, I'm not going to be a manager again. I thought Lily was going to faint when I broke the news."

"She's the older one, right?"

I nodded. "She's been there since 1975. I'm not sure she's even worked anywhere else. It's not like she can afford to retire yet either. She's on her own and really needs the money."

Greg sighed. "Why do you think I work for myself now? At least if I go down, I know who to blame." He struck a dramatic pose. "I'm in charge of my own destiny."

Despite my sadness, I cracked a smile. Greg was doing his best to cheer me up and I loved him for it.

He refilled my glass from the bottle of Merlot on the dining table and handed it to me. I took a large gulp.

"Anyway," he said, "about this holiday. How about Scotland? That island we always said we'd visit. Arnsay is it?"

Arnsay. I'd drooled over photographs of the dramatic landscape of mountains sweeping down to the sea, the history that went back to prehistoric times, with stone circles, Viking treasures and a quaint little town. A place to heal, reflect and refresh the spirit. Perfect.

"What do you say then? They have Broadband and Wi-Fi now, so I can take my laptop and work pretty much as well from there as I can here. We could go tomorrow if you like."

I didn't need to be asked again, although, God help me, I wish I had. I wish now with all my heart I'd insisted we go somewhere else, as far away from that island as possible. As if it would have made any difference. But two days later, with hotel and flights booked and bags packed, we started our journey on a spring-like April day.

After a change of planes in Inverness, we eventually landed in a small jet on Arnsay's single landing strip, where a minibus transported its passengers to the center of the main town, also called, unimaginatively, Arnsay.

Arnsay, Arnsay, so good they named it twice.

The walk to the hotel took us off the main thoroughfare, down a quiet side street that meandered and then widened. The Arnsay Hotel's white walls and bright blue paintwork gleamed in the late afternoon sun.

"Make the most of it." Our charming host beamed as he spoke in his lilting local accent that sounded more Scandinavian than Scottish. "It'll be raining again tomorrow. Normal service will be resumed."

As I smiled and shook his hand, images of a genial Hercule Poirot flashed through my mind. Or more accurately, David Suchet's version of Poirot. Laurence McGregor was of similar stature and bustled along with equally short steps. He insisted on carrying our cases up a narrow flight of stairs, along a winding corridor, through three fire doors, until we finally arrived—a little breathless—outside Room 9. Laurence inserted an electronic card key.

"You'll be comfortable in here." Was that an assurance or an order? I smiled. He acknowledged it.

Inside smelled sweetly of the spring flowers in the vase that decorated the room in a splash of pink, red, blue and yellow. I admired the mahogany four-poster bed and matching furniture. This was a well-cared-for, comfortable room. I looked through the window, where the view stretched clear across to the lake some distance away.

"Now the ensuite is just here." Laurence opened a door and an electric light and fan immediately kicked in. Inside was all gleaming chrome, brilliant white fittings and sparkling glass. Greg would be pleased. He hated showers, and this bathroom came equipped with a good size bath, just right for his daily wallow.

Laurence moved on from the ensuite and pointed to a tray covered with a box of Twining specialty teas and at least three types of coffee. A small kettle and two mugs stood at the ready.

"Now, if you want anything else, just pick up the phone and dial '0'. There are some leaflets here, with local information." He indicated a small wooden rack on the desk. "And the Wi-Fi details are right next to it. I see you'll be wanting to use it." He pointed at Greg's laptop case, which now lay on the bed.

"Yes," Greg said.

"That's no problem at all. It's free of charge, so just go online whenever you want to." He said it as if the internet remained an alien concept to him—an impression he then compounded with his next words. "I'm hopeless with the internet. Simply useless. I really am. I leave all that sort of thing to Terry, my partner. I so admire people who know how to work that thing. Anyway, I'll love you and leave you now, but don't forget to call if you need anything. Dinner's from seven until nine and breakfast is from seven-thirty to nine-thirty. Enjoy your stay with us." He beamed and closed the door behind him.

I stared out of the window again. "It's a lovely room isn't it? And the view..." We were at the back of the hotel and immediately outside and below, a neatly laid out patio and garden led onto a small car park, beyond which a stretch of grass trailed down to the lake. It shimmered as the sunlight bounced off the ripples of its peaceful waters. As I stood and watched, I felt my tensions easing and I inhaled deeply.

A couple of oystercatchers took off and soared over the lake, before disappearing from sight, and it seemed nothing could disturb the tranquility of this landscape.

When I glanced back at the lakeshore, a figure had appeared, dressed in a long gown, but too far away to make out any detail. For some reason I couldn't grasp, goosebumps rose on my skin and I shivered, despite the warmth of the room. I looked down at my arms, rubbed them and when I looked up again, the figure had gone.

By the time I tore myself away from the window, Greg was already deep in concentration, checking emails. Exclamations of "Good grief", "What the hell has he done now?" and exasperated sighs punctured the air. The life of a business consultant can be a frustrating one.

I looked at my watch. Six o'clock. An hour till dinner and plenty of time for a leisurely shower, once I unpacked.

Ten minutes later, as I luxuriated in the cascading hot water, I reflected on what a brilliant idea all this had been. Looking back, I'm glad I didn't have an inkling of what was to come, because it was too late by then, too late to turn back and go home. Kismet, fate, call it what you will, was already cranking up the handle and I'm glad I had a few more days of relative innocence.

Dinner consisted of a delicious home-made steak and ale pie. Greg and I were both tired out after our long trip and went to bed early. I sank gratefully into the welcoming bed and, in the quiet room, I fell asleep almost immediately. But I awoke to the hammering of rain on the window.

Greg pulled back the curtains, letting in gray light. "Not a day for sightseeing."

"How about the museum?"

Greg frowned. "Actually I've got a lot of work on. The builder's in a mess again and I need to sort it out. Would you be okay to go on your own? We could meet up here for lunch and, if the rain's lifted, we could go for a walk this afternoon. I should be on top of it by then."

I nodded and he smiled, with relief no doubt. A love of museums was the other thing we didn't share. That and my specter.

At the thought of her, I wondered if she would follow me here. She had traveled with me as I had moved from my parents' home to student house-share, then rented flat and marital home, but if she followed me on holiday, that would be a first. But then, why would she need to? In this idyllic spot, we were here to relax, not become involved in anything traumatic.

At breakfast, I flicked through the leaflet on the museum. Housed in the former home of the wealthy Devine family, it contained many of the possessions of its last owner, Jonas Devine, who had inherited his wealth from land held by his family in Ireland for generations. Jonas, I learned, was an eccentric, and an ardent collector of cameos, among other things. Well, *that* would keep me out of mischief for an hour or so on a rainy morning.

Classical piano music wafted into the blue and white dining room. I guessed Laurence and Terry must be keen on Wedgwood pottery, judging by the decorations and the various small vases lined up along the mantelpiece.

Laurence placed golden toast on a table already bursting with two full Scottish breakfasts and their associated condiments. He saw me looking at the leaflet.

"Aye, there's more there than you might think. The leaflet really doesn't do it justice." He clapped his small hands together. "I've told them. Let Terry do it and he'll make a far better job of it. Have you seen our website?"

Between mouthfuls of bacon, I nodded as I remembered the fussy, over-wordy site, broken links and exasperating tendency to ping you back to the home page no matter where you intended to go.

Laurence shook his head. "They won't listen of course, but that's typical council for you."

Greg raised and lowered his eyebrows in a gesture I had seen many times over the years. Whether Laurence picked up on his irritation, I don't know, but he smiled, said, "Enjoy your breakfast," and moved on to the next table.

Greg leaned forward and whispered to me. "I really have to meet this Terry."

I giggled and bit into my toast.

Greg finished his breakfast and reached for the coffeepot. "I'd better use the residents' lounge today or I'll be turfed out when they come to do the room."

"Good idea."

Greg downed his coffee and pushed his chair away.

"Ready for your history lesson?" He grinned.

I swiped him with my napkin. "Philistine."

Wrapped in a raincoat, I left the hotel, and the waterproof Barbour hat I crammed on my head struggled to contain my long hair. As I stepped out onto the street, a couple of hikers passed by, equipped with serious boots, rucksacks and weather-beaten faces. No mere downpour of rain would deter *them*.

I turned in the opposite direction and wished the rain wouldn't soak my face. No point risking an umbrella though. The wind would have it inside out in no time.

Just then, an elderly man came towards me.

"Good morning," he said.

"Morning,"

"Don't worry. It'll clear up later. You can see a little patch of blue sky, over the lake there."

"I hope so," I said, but he was already on his way. I carried on past a row of old cottages, until the street opened up into a square.

On the right were more homes and, on the left, a grand stone-built house stood three stories high, with Georgian windows and door.

An old sign read, 'Arnsay Museum' while, below it, worn by many years of wind, sun and rain, the words, 'Arnsay House' were etched in stone, over the doorway.

The lake lay closer here than it had been at the hotel. Gray, lonely and cold beneath rain-sodden clouds. So much for local knowledge; that patch of blue sky was already history.

I climbed the couple of steps and turned the door handle. Inside, a clutter of tall glass cabinets competed for my attention. 'Prehistoric Arnsay', 'Agriculture in Arnsay', 'Medieval Arnsay' and others too numerous to take in at first. A homely, old-fashioned smell of wood and polish filled the air.

"Good morning to you." A man in his forties or fifties peered at me from behind black-rimmed glasses.

"Good morning," I said.

I paid my entrance fee, managing to find a space for my money on a counter littered with postcards, fridge magnets, guide books, leaflets and souvenir pens.

"You start over there," he pointed at 'Prehistoric Arnsay', "and then move around in a clockwise direction. When you get to 'Arnsay and Whaling', you'll see the figure of Archibald Strangelove. Behind him is a flight of stairs that will take you up to the Devine Collection. Enjoy your visit. If you need any help, just let me know."

"Thank you," I said. His badge read 'Duncan Stout, Curator' and his smile exuded warmth. Duncan Stout clearly enjoyed his work.

The museum was locked in a time-warp of what museums used to be in my childhood. Cabinet after cabinet displayed an array of flint arrowheads, primitive jewelry, bone, antler picks and tiny unrecognizable fragments of clothing, preserved in the peat bogs for five thousand years. They even boasted a mock burial. The skeleton lay in a fetal position and looked a little too realistic for me, so I moved on.

Eventually I met Archibald Strangelove who stood on the prow of a boat, swathed in moth-eaten furs. The faded sign described him as a, 'famous Arctic explorer who mysteriously drowned after being rescued by a whaling ship on October 19th 1878.' Sad to say, I had never heard of him.

His weather-beaten face was pockmarked by little bits of chipped off plaster of Paris. You need a bit of an overhaul, old son, I thought, and then started up the stairs.

Fourteen steps took me up one floor and then I opened a door that would lead me to where I am today.

Would to God I had stayed downstairs.

Chapter Two

My footsteps echoed as I trod the creaky polished floorboards in the empty room. I couldn't overcome the feeling of being watched. For the second time since I had arrived on Arnsay, goosebumps rose along my arms and the little hairs on the back of my neck stood up. Don't be ridiculous, I told myself, your imagination's got the better of you again.

I shook my head and made for the nearest glass cabinet. Above it, a portrait of the museum's benefactor—Jonas Devine—gazed out at the world. I studied his face for a minute. His dark hair, flecked with gray, receded at the temples. He had a kind expression, clear brown eyes and a neatly trimmed moustache in the style of the late Victorians. My attention returned to his eyes. The artist had captured an ethereal, faraway look in them as if his subject could see something beyond what had been in the room. He was dressed in a dark suit of the period and one hand rested on his thigh, while the other held a book. I peered closer but couldn't see any title. Maybe it was a small Bible or perhaps a novel by his favorite writer.

I switched my gaze down to the contents of the cabinet. A pair of wire-rimmed spectacles, gloves, a pen and inkstand, all personal items from the man's study. I moved on and came across an information board nailed to the wall. It seemed Jonas Devine had bought the house when he brought his new bride Margarita—a former music hall artist—to settle on this remote island. This had followed some unspecified need of hers to leave Edinburgh, where she worked, and where she first met Jonas. A photograph showed a dark-eyed woman dressed in Spanish style, complete with mantilla and fan. I could imagine her dancing Flamenco, flashing brown legs as she laughed and flirted with every man she saw.

Another photo showed a slightly older Margarita with a little boy of around two— her son, Adrian. Her eyes no longer flashed and the Latin flamboyance had given way to a demure dress, well suited to a young Victorian mother. But I read defiance in her expression. I bet she could be a handful, I thought.

I read on. Margarita had died soon after giving birth to her second son, Robert, leaving Jonas with two young boys. In 1897, he had acquired a governess—Agnes Morrison—a widow with a young daughter. They were married soon after. There was one photograph of her, with Jonas's two sons, but no sign of her daughter. I did learn one thing about her though. Her name was Grace and she took Jonas's surname on her mother's marriage. Grace Devine.

An icy breeze chilled me, and I hugged myself. I had the strongest feeling of someone standing right by my shoulder, but I had heard no one come up the stairs. I braced myself, took a deep breath and whirled around, relieved to see I was still alone. But then another sound drifted towards me. A sigh. Again I told myself to stop imagining things and carried on wandering around the rooms.

Jonas Devine had certainly been an avid collector. Stamps, coins, butterflies, all cataloged in meticulous detail and laid out for inspection. I supposed there wasn't much else to do if you were independently wealthy and lived on a remote Scottish island in the late nineteenth century.

One room was devoted to his collection of stuffed birds and animals, all presented in glass cases, in an approximation of their real habitat. Goodness alone knew where he had displayed all these things when he was alive. I found them hideous and macabre, but then I've never been a fan of taxidermy.

Below each case was a chest of shallow drawers. I opened one and found a collection of cameos. Much more my taste, and he had some lovely ones too. Some were carved onto coral, others onto tortoiseshell, some on ebony and some ivory. Some were the traditional profile, but most were far more intricate, and I pulled out drawer after drawer of them, all laid out under glass. The collection must have numbered hundreds, maybe thousands, and as for their value…

In the second chest, one drawer stuck halfway and wouldn't budge, and I could tell something was wedged inside.

I reached in and poked around until I found the culprit. A material that felt like canvas was firmly stuck there. I pushed at it but it wouldn't shift, so I wiggled it around and tried to grab hold of it. Eventually it gave and I pulled out something that looked like a rolled up painting.

I unrolled it and revealed a strange picture. The bizarre subject was painted in blue-green hues, and represented either a lake or the sea, from underwater. In the foreground a girl floated. Her eyes were closed and I guessed she was around fourteen or fifteen years old. She was dressed in a white gown, decorated with a pattern of tiny flowers. Her feet were shod in black Victorian, buttoned-up boots and the gown billowed up from her ankles, exposing white stockings. Her hands floated next to her and her light brown hair flowed loose around her. With a pang, I realized the artist hadn't depicted a living subject. This girl had drowned.

It could almost have been a photograph, and I had the strongest urge to touch the girl and stroke her hair, but my fingers found the unmistakable texture of oil paint.

The goosebumps arose for the third time but I ignored them, riveted by the loving attention to detail in the artist's tragic subject. Who would paint such a picture? I searched around for a signature but couldn't find one.

I don't know how long I stared. The painting troubled, repelled and fascinated me all in one go. Finally, I decided to take it down to Duncan. He could find a more suitable home for it. Then, as I started to roll it up, the girl's eyes opened.

With a cry, I dropped the painting on the floor, where it quickly rolled itself back up again. I backed away. It had to be my overactive imagination again. I had stared at the picture for too long and, rather like scrying in a mirror, my mind had played a trick on me.

The minutes ticked by while the painting remained static on the floor and I examined my options. To get out of this room, I would have to go past it. The canvas lay right in front of the only exit. I could either leave it there, where anyone could find and maybe even steal it, or I could put it back in the drawer and forget I'd ever seen the bloody thing. Or I could continue with my original plan and take it down to Duncan.

I shuddered at the last option. The thought of carrying that thing all the way down the stairs filled me with dread. I really didn't want to touch it again.

Leaving it on the floor seemed preferable, but what if it was valuable? Unlikely, or else it wouldn't have been stuffed in a drawer, but maybe they'd forgotten about it. Or perhaps it was some priceless heirloom they had been searching for over the years, never dreaming for one moment that it lay there all this time. When had that drawer last been opened? For all I knew it could have been tucked away, undisturbed, since before Jonas Devine died.

I looked at my watch. Eleven forty-five. I needed to make up my mind and get back to the hotel to meet Greg for lunch. In a flash, I took a deep breath and lunged for the painting.

It was rolled up too loosely to slip back into the drawer, so, holding my breath, I unrolled it and prayed that when I looked, the girl's eyes would be closed. Thank God, they were. Maybe I really had imagined it.

I rolled the picture into a narrow tube and slipped it back into the front of the drawer where it sat, snugly, allowing me to close the drawer over it.

I retraced my steps back to the stairs, still with the uncomfortable feeling of being watched. As I put my foot on the first step, I heard the sigh again and my heart pounded as I raced down the stairs.

"Goodbye. Thank you," Duncan called after me as I hurried out of the door.

I smiled and waved at him and hoped he didn't think I was rude.

Outside, I leaned against the wall for a moment, panting. The rain had cleared and a couple of hikers looked at me curiously as they passed. I smiled in an effort to reassure them I wasn't having a heart attack and they smiled back and continued on their way.

I started back towards the hotel, my brain swamped with questions, explanations that didn't quite work and yet more questions. All the while, the image of that drowned girl's eyes haunted me. Something had happened up there in that gallery and I couldn't escape the feeling that a connection had been made and this was just the start.

"Enjoy your trip to the museum this morning?" In the café, with its comforting aromas of freshly brewed coffee and newly baked bread, Greg bit into his ham and brie ciabatta. Meanwhile, I tried to work up enthusiasm for carrot and coriander soup and a whole grain roll. It smelled delicious, but my mind was still too preoccupied to care much about food.

"Yes," I replied, trying to sound my usual self. "It's very old fashioned, but that seems right for the island, somehow."

"See anything interesting?"

Greg was eyeing me rather too intently for my liking. I lowered my eyes and concentrated on getting my soup to my mouth without shaking it out of the spoon.

"There's a figure representing a famous Arctic explorer called Archibald Strangelove. Poor man looks as if he's been attacked by a gang of moths on a night out. And half his nose is dropping off."

"Maybe he had leprosy."

I smiled. "Nah. He was drowned mysteriously apparently."

"You know, if I was going to be drowned, I'd like it to be mysteriously."

I laughed with Greg but, into my mind, yet again, flashed the painting and, once again, I shivered.

"You cold?" Greg asked. "We could go back to the hotel and grab you a jumper or thicker jacket or something."

"No, I'm fine, really. Shall we go for a walk down by the lake this afternoon? It looked so peaceful yesterday and now the sun's coming out, it should be lovely down there."

"Good idea. I've finished my stuff for the day and I came prepared."

He thrust out his left foot, clad in a sensible walking boot.

"Great. Walking's big business around here. I saw some very serious hikers around this morning."

"They were probably going up to the mountain," Greg said between sips of coffee. "It's named after your explorer. Strangelove. I thought it was an odd name for a mountain until you told me you'd seen the old guy. By the way, Laurence brought me coffee in the lounge this morning and stopped for a chat." He rolled his eyes and drained his cup.

"Don't tell me, half an hour later—"

"You've got it. That man can talk for Scotland, but I learned a few things, although you probably saw it all in the museum. Did you read about the Devine family?"

I nodded. "Bits. Jonas Devine collected everything from coins to cameos, stuffed a whole load of unsuspecting animals and birds, and married twice."

"Yep. That's what Laurence told me too. Did you read anything about his stepdaughter, Grace?"

"Not very much. Just her name really."

Greg smiled. "Oh, you'll like this. She's supposed to haunt the place, especially around the lake. Apparently she drowned there in 1902 and rumor has it that it was no accident."

Now he had my attention. I moved forward. "Really? What else did Laurence tell you?"

"Well, apparently Jonas's eldest son, Adrian, was bitterly jealous of his stepsister and one January day, he was with her when she drowned. His younger brother, Robert, was also there and he spilled the beans to daddy, who then banished Adrian from the island and he was never heard of again. In fact, if you go on the internet and do a search for Adrian Devine, you'll come up with precisely zilch. Curiosity got the better of me and I Googled him. Nothing. It's as if he never existed."

"Wow! And is this all true?"

Greg nodded. "You ask Laurence. He thought he'd seen Grace's ghost, but Terry told him it was just the moonlight on the water, casting shadows. I don't think Laurence is convinced, but Terry was probably right."

He seemed about to say more and I was sure, "Because there's no such thing as ghosts" was about to spill from his lips. It wouldn't be the first time. But, right now I could tell, Greg was trying hard not to do, or say, anything to offend or upset me. I loved him for it, but it didn't really make any difference. I knew him so well. I knew his skepticism of anything he couldn't prove with one or more of his senses. Nevertheless, I smiled. I may even have nodded.

We paid the bill, left the little café and headed for the lakeside. The breeze had dropped, the air tasted fresh and clean, and puffy marshmallow clouds had replaced the leaden, gray sky.

"It's turning into a lovely afternoon," I said as I tucked my arm into the crook of Greg's elbow. He squeezed my hand and a rush of emotion swept through me. I reminded myself how lucky I was to have found him.

As we neared the lake, grass gave way to scrubland and sloped down to a narrow patch of shingle, lapped by the water. Fulmars, teals and Arctic terns soared, glided and swooped. They dived every now and then, leaving only their bottoms above water. On the shore, oystercatchers, with their distinctive orange beaks, foraged for food.

Greg and I stood by the water's edge, drinking in the tranquility.

"It's beautiful here, isn't it?" I whispered, not wanting to disturb the stillness.

"Mm," he said. "I'm glad we came, are you?"

"Yes." At that moment, I truly meant it. Arnsay was a place for restful reflection and right now, that's what we were doing.

We ambled along the edge of the lake and stopped now and then to examine an unusual tiny flower or watch the graceful flight of an arctic tern.

"I love their tail feathers," I said as one hovered far above us. "That incredible "V' shape. Do you suppose it makes them more aero-dynamic or something? Oh, that one's caught something." I pointed up at a tern that had just taken off from the lake.

"He'd better watch it. Look at that bird there."

I gasped as I saw a larger bird, a skua I think, swoop down on the tern and grab the fish out of its mouth. The shock of the assault sent the bird plummeting downwards and we watched—in my case, horrified—as the poor creature tumbled. Just in time, it seemed to come to its senses and rose again. But this time, it flew off in the opposite direction to the marauding skua.

I cupped my hands and shouted at the fast disappearing interloper, "*Bully.*"

Greg laughed. "If he heard you he's probably doing the avian equivalent of sticking two fingers up at you."

"*And up yours too!*" I called to the bird.

Greg was almost beside himself and I collapsed into giggles too. We were like a couple of carefree teenagers.

"Come on," he said at last, "I'll buy you an ice cream."

Arm in arm, we left the lakeside and headed back to the town center. At one point, I turned and looked back at where we had watched the tern and the skua. Someone stood there now, looking out over the lake. A young girl, all alone and dressed in a white gown. I stopped, unable to believe my eyes.

"What's the matter?"

I looked back at Greg. "I'm not sure…I…Do you see a girl standing over there…" I turned back.

"What girl? Where?" He stared around at the now empty landscape.

"Never mind," I said and, to avoid any discussion, added, "I made a mistake. Just a trick of the light."

I awoke suddenly in the middle of the night and listened. The only sound came from Greg's rhythmical breathing as he slept on, next to me.

I decided perhaps a trip to the bathroom would settle me down again. I went, returned and slipped under the covers. Greg was still asleep and, after some minutes, I drifted off.

I dreamed of the lake, the blue-green water lapping the shore. A lonely girl in a long white dress, speckled with tiny flowers, gazed far out into the distance. My dream mind told me not to approach her, but my feet wouldn't obey and I drew closer. I could almost touch her. Her light brown hair was caught up in an old-fashioned bun at the nape of her neck. Little wisps of it had escaped from its clips and fluttered in the breeze. In her hand, she held the ribbons of a fur-trimmed hat, so pristine it had to be new.

Suddenly she spun around and I gasped at the sight of her large, blue, desperate eyes. In my dream mind, I heard her, and the longing and loneliness in her voice tugged at me.

I have waited for so long. Now, at last, you are here. None of the others would listen, but you can hear me. Please help me. You have to find him. He has to forgive me.

"Find who?" I said. "Who has to forgive you?"

Adrian.

I shot out of my dream and sat, bolt upright, as tears streamed down my face.

My sudden movement woke Greg. "Whatever's the matter, Alex? You look as if you've had the nightmare to end all nightmares."

How right, I thought, but didn't say so. He held me close as I recovered myself. And then I knew I had to find out more about Grace Devine. At the same time, I realized why my specter had come to me when she did. Losing my job wasn't the momentous event she had tried to warn me about. It was this. But I could never attempt to explain it to Greg. How could I tell him that some long-dead girl, who had been waiting for someone to help her, had latched on to me because, after who knows how many attempts, she had finally found someone who had the ability to listen to her? He'd have me committed! No, I would have to handle this myself. And I hadn't a clue how to go about it.

For once, I was glad of the lashing rain. It gave Greg the perfect excuse to carry on working and me an obvious reason to return to the museum. Out on the sodden streets, only intrepid hikers strode past. A couple of forlorn cats, huddled together under a hedge, mewled as I hurried past them. Normally I would have stopped and stroked them, but I had far too much on my mind for that.

I carried my large handbag, slung over my shoulder. Inside was a notebook and pen. I had some vague idea of talking to the curator and finding out more about the family who lived there, especially Grace and how she died. I also wanted to gather up courage to look at that painting again, although the thought of it sent tremors of fear curling around my nerves.

"Good morning again. How nice to see you back." Duncan's cheery greeting gave me confidence and reassurance at a time when I truly needed it.

"Good morning," I said. "I thought I'd carry on where I left off yesterday. It's too wet to do any sightseeing and I was right in the middle of something."

"Ah, you ran out of time. I wondered why you dashed out."

I almost told him the real reason. Would he think I was mad? Probably. I dismissed the thought and merely nodded. "I wondered if you could tell me a little more about the family who lived here."

"The Devines? Oh yes, indeed. I'd be happy to. What would you like to know?"

I rummaged in my bag for my notebook and pen, while Duncan came out from behind his counter. He indicated a coffee table and chairs and we sat.

"I'm curious about the family set up. Jonas Devine married twice, didn't he?"

Duncan nodded. He reached up and ran his fingers along a shelf of albums until he came to the one he was looking for. As he opened it, I could see it was full of old sepia and black and white photographs.

He flicked through a few leaves and then laid the album flat on the table in front of us. Then he pointed at a photograph of a face I recognized from the day before. "That's Jonas Devine," he said. "His family were wealthy landowners, particularly in Ireland, but they also owned this island and some valuable sheep farming areas in Scotland, as well as some fancy property in Edinburgh."

"So Jonas didn't need to pursue a career then?"

Duncan shook his head. "No. He went to university, but after that he drifted for some years, did the Grand Tour of Europe, came back to Edinburgh and met, and fell in love with, Margarita Garcia Lopez." He pointed at a photo similar to the one I had seen upstairs, in all her Spanish finery.

"She looks very beautiful," I said. "And look at those flashing eyes. You can just imagine her sweeping poor old Jonas off his feet."

Duncan laughed. "Well, she would have seemed far more exotic than anything else he'd seen in Edinburgh, I should imagine."

"She was a music hall performer wasn't she? A dancer?"

"Not entirely. Oh, she certainly performed in the music halls and she was known to dance, traditional Spanish folk dances, Flamenco and so on. But her main claim to fame, or more accurately, infamy, was her mindreading act."

"*Mindreading?*"

"Yes, indeed. She quickly became known for the accuracy of her readings and her ability to predict the future. At first she just tacked it on to her dance hall routine, but soon she became so much in demand, she ditched the dancing altogether. She could make far more money from small group sessions in her flat and she could hardly keep up with demand at one point, so she held them twice daily and soon moved up to the smart part of town and became one of Jonas's tenants."

"So that's how they met?"

"Aye. By now she could afford his rents and, of course, by moving up town, she was able to attract a far more respectable and well-heeled clientele."

"So why on earth would someone earning pots of money and enjoying a lavish lifestyle in Edinburgh want to closet herself away on a remote island like this? Even if her husband did own it. Or was Jonas some sort of a recluse?"

Duncan smiled and flicked over a few more pages before continuing.

"Here comes the interesting part," he said and pointed to a faded, yellowing newspaper cutting. A photograph of Margarita stared out from the page. Her set lips might be defiant, but she had fear in her eyes. I read the headline. "Famed psychic chief suspect in Dundee Street murder."

"Oh, good Lord! Was she convicted?"

"Oh, no. The charges were spurious at best. In one of her sittings, she predicted that someone present at the time would meet death at the hands of a stranger and when Lord Carthew was robbed and strangled the very next evening, the police came knocking on her door. She soon discovered that the very clients she regarded as her friends were only too ready to disassociate themselves from her at the merest whiff of scandal. Even though she could prove she was elsewhere at the time and had nothing to gain from his death, the only person to stand by her was Jonas Devine. They were married a month later and moved immediately to Arnsay, where she lived for the rest of her life."

I stared down at the picture and then at subsequent photos of the lady in question. I hadn't taken to her on first impression, but now I began to feel sorry for her.

"She doesn't look very happy. I suppose isolation didn't suit her."

"No, indeed. Margarita was always one for the bright lights and attention. But don't feel too sorry for her. Remember that Jonas gave up his life for her as well. And he didn't have an easy time with her. Servants reported terrible rows, broken glassware and plates, and poor old Jonas dashing out of the house, shaking his head and dabbing his face with a handkerchief where she'd clawed him. She was quite a vixen, you know."

Another page along, a photo of Margarita and her baby son peered out at me.

"Ah, now that's Adrian," Duncan said, tapping at the image. "Margarita doted on him. He inherited her dark hair, olive skin and black eyes and, unfortunately, her insane jealousy and temper. He was subject to tantrums if he didn't get his own way, which he always did with his mother.

"Nanny after nanny came and went, unable to tolerate Adrian's behavior and his mother's defensive temper. She would never acknowledge that her son was capable of any misdemeanor, nor would she allow him out of her sight for more than a couple of hours at a time.

"After she died, soon after Robert's birth, Jonas engaged a nanny for the little boy and a succession of governesses for Adrian. The last of these was Agnes and, by all accounts, she would stand no nonsense from Adrian. She won Jonas's heart and they were married, but it wasn't to last. Barely a year later, Agnes caught some kind of fever and died."

"That's such a sad story."

"Aye, it is, and not without its mysteries too. Folk here have always been quite superstitious and, at the time, there were rumors about Agnes's sudden death. The fever she contracted was an unusual strain that had the doctors baffled. Jonas Devine even brought in a specialist from Aberdeen, but he couldn't isolate it. Pretty soon, the gossipmongers were whispering that Adrian had something to do with it."

"Adrian? But he was just a young boy."

"Indeed, but some people believed his mother was some kind of witch and had passed some of her, shall we call them, gifts, on to her son. As she lay dying, Margarita's last wish had been to see Adrian. He was brought to her and she grabbed the bairn and clung on to him while she whispered nonstop in his ear for something like half an hour. Then she released her hold and died. Just like that." Duncan snapped his fingers.

"And Adrian witnessed this? His mother dying?"

"Horrifying, isn't it? He was just seven years old and I think it probably explains quite a lot about his subsequent behavior. That and the way his mother had spoiled him in the first place."

The door opened and four tourists dashed in from the rain, shaking themselves and showering the entrance way.

Duncan stood. "I'm sorry, I'll need to look after these customers. I'll be back as soon as I can."

"No, it's fine. You've been very helpful, thank you. I'll just go through this album and then I'll go back upstairs and carry on looking at the collection."

Duncan hesitated and I wondered if he was about to say something, but then thought better of it. Instead, he smiled and greeted his customers.

I turned over page after page. Pictures of Margarita and her son gave way to photos of Agnes and her stepsons, charting their progress as they grew up.

Then I turned over a page and, staring up at me was a face I shouldn't have recognized, not if dreams were just figments of imagination and ghosts were tricks of the light.

A slim girl with long hair tied back in a ponytail, stood, her hands clasped demurely in front of her. She wore a high-necked, long-sleeved, lacy blouse and around her neck was an attractive oval locket that looked like silver. Her eyes gazed out at me and I didn't need to read the caption. Grace Devine. This might be the first time I had officially seen her picture, but I would have recognized her anywhere. She was the girl in my dream, the girl at the lake shore—and the drowned girl in the painting.

At that moment, I knew what I had to do. I closed the album and returned it to the shelf. Duncan was still busy with his customers, who had evidently just arrived on the ferry and needed somewhere to stay for the night. He recommended our hotel, so maybe I would see them at dinner.

I remember all these thoughts idling through my brain. I remember using them to calm my racing heartbeat. I also remember how I failed. By the time I reached the top of the stairs, I wanted to race back down them. I hesitated, aware of my own breathing. Too fast. I struggled to slow it right down. Deep calm breaths.

I dared let go of the banister, reassured by the murmurs of indistinct conversation and laughter wafting up from downstairs. At least it broke the heavy silence that flooded this part of the building.

I looked down at my trainers and forced myself to place one foot in front of the other. I reached the chest of drawers where I had replaced the painting, and grasped the brass handles with both hands. One swift tug and the drawer slid open.

There lay the picture. My hands trembled as I felt the linen-like texture of the canvas and removed it from the drawer. This time, no sigh sounded in my ear. No goosebumps rose on my arms. Just me and the painting, the picture no one seemed to know or care about. No one would miss it, would they? I unrolled it.

The water still looked so real, my fingers should get wet simply by touching it. And the drowned girl still floated, with her eyes closed, exactly as I had first seen her. Her features were Grace's in every detail. I could imagine that hair in a long ponytail, or tied up in a neat bun with just a few wisps escaping and fluttering in the breeze. I had never felt maternal before, but now, all I wanted was to take that poor girl in my arms and hug her, hold her, keep her safe. Yet she was beyond saving. In this life at any rate.

I have no explanation for what I did next. As a youngster, I shrank from childish pranks, refusing even to steal midget gems from the corner shop as all my school friends were doing. I didn't care that they called me names and mocked me for it. Stealing was just plain wrong and that's all there was to it. So what rationale I could have for rolling up a possibly valuable painting and thrusting it into my bag, I cannot imagine, but that's what I did. Then I forced myself to amble down the stairs, say a cheerful and innocent goodbye to Duncan and leave the museum, heart pounding and hands shaking.

The rain still sheeted down and I crammed my hat firmly on my head, aware of strands of wet hair as they slapped against my cheeks.

I checked my bag was firmly zipped. I didn't want the painting to get wet, as I fully intended to return it in the state in which I had found it. Just not today and possibly not for a number of days. Something told me the picture might be key in solving Grace's mystery.

Instead of making for the café where I was due to meet Greg for lunch, I went round the other side of the museum and made for the lake. In the distance, I could see the girl and I had the strongest impression she was waiting for me. I had to go to her.

I shivered and pulled my raincoat closer around me. My jeans were soaked dark blue and rain blurred my vision. For an instant, I thought I saw something else standing next to the girl. Something gray, shadowy and familiar. My specter. But that was impossible, I told myself.

Now a chilly breeze blew through me. I really should have been getting back, but I couldn't. She knew I was there and I couldn't let her down. She seemed so sad and desperate, so I pressed on, speeding up my stride, amazed that the terror I had felt had largely dissolved.

Six feet away from her, I stopped.

"Grace?" My voice wavered. I coughed and tried again. "Grace, I'm here to help you. I have the painting."

As if in slow motion, she began to turn and all my fear swept back. What would she be like? This wraith or whatever she had become.

But I simply saw the girl in the photograph. She shimmered a little and her color was pale; one white hand clutched at the silver locket around her neck. Her dress and hat were not as bright as they would have been in life, but her blue eyes were clear. They weren't hollow like my specter's and when she spoke, her lips parted to show even teeth. Her words floated into my brain, as if she was lip synching to a track in my head.

You must find Adrian. I died with a curse on my lips and I must be forgiven. Adrian must forgive me.

Once again, I had the strongest urge to hold her as if she was my own child. "Adrian's dead, Grace. This is 2014 and he couldn't possibly be alive. Do you know where he went after he left the island? Did he have any children?"

She continued to fix me with that haunted gaze.

Please help me. I've waited for so long…

That was all it took for me to realize I couldn't ignore her. It was too late for that.

The rain slowed to a drizzle, then stopped and the sun came out. As it did so, she faded from view, but the bond between us was sealed. She had chosen me because out of all the people she had appeared to over the years, I alone could hear her. Maybe another bond drew us together too, but I didn't know what it was then. But I did know I couldn't turn away from her. I would never forgive myself for deserting her when she needed my help so desperately. God help me.

———

A few minutes passed and she didn't return, so I headed back to the hotel, with just enough time to get to our room and change out of my wet things. I needed a hiding place for the picture. I wasn't ready to try and explain my moment of madness to Greg. He would certainly march me right back to the museum with a fervent apology and a plausible explanation.

Until I had my secret stashed away, I wasn't ready to meet him, so I avoided the residents' lounge and prayed he was hard at work there, in front of his laptop. As soon as I opened our bedroom door, I was relieved to see I must be right, as the room was empty.

After a quick shower, I dried my hair and applied fresh make up. Now comfortably changed into dry jeans, flat shoes and light sweater, I steadied my hand, ready to apply eyeliner. Job done, I stepped back and appraised my appearance. I certainly didn't look like a thief who talked to ghosts and, providing I could keep it to myself, Greg would never know how I had really spent my morning.

With ten minutes to go before I was due to meet him, I still needed to find my hiding place. I looked around the room. It was no good putting it in any of the drawers, as Greg was quite likely to open them.

The wardrobe. On the top shelf lay spare blankets and pillows. He surely wouldn't need to go rummaging up there.

I crossed to it and opened the double doors. If I tucked the painting firmly under the spare blanket and pushed it as far in as I could, it should be out of sight and lay undisturbed until I was ready to do something with it.

I grabbed my bag and removed the canvas. I needed it to stay tightly rolled up so it would take up less space and remain inconspicuous. The last thing I wanted was for Greg to open the wardrobe and have a stolen painting topple out at him.

I rummaged in my purse and found the elastic band I sometimes used to tie back my hair. Without unrolling the painting again, I wound the band around it three times, securing it firmly. I then stretched up and shoved it as far under the blanket as possible. No one would ever guess anything was under there. Satisfied, I closed the doors, took my bag and coat and went to meet Greg.

We spent the rest of the afternoon wandering around the town, buying postcards and the odd souvenir T-shirt. We drank coffee in the little café, wrote the cards and posted them, all normal tourist activities in a quiet island town. Greg seemed happy and relaxed and I pretended I was too, because I knew how much it meant to him. But my mind kept churning over how I could help Grace, and every mental path I took led me nowhere. I came up against the same barrier—lack of information—and I knew I must speak with Duncan again.

Grace had said I must find her stepbrother who, like her, must have been dead for many years. But I had to find where he had gone. Even if he didn't come up in any internet searches, somewhere there must be a record of his life after he left Arnsay and, if I was ever going to save Grace Devine, I had to find it.

Chapter Three

"You needn't think that just because you're Bull's pet, you're anything special."

Grace studied her black button boots as Adrian, her stepbrother, spat out the words. Her heart thumped in her chest as he moved closer and she dared to look up. She saw his flashing dark eyes, unruly mop of black hair and the mouth, twisted by rage. He always wore that expression when angry with her, although for the life of her she hadn't the slightest idea what she had done to offend him.

"Don't be such a bully, Adrian."

Grace's attention shot from one brother to the other. Robert, four years her junior, hardly looked or behaved like Adrian. No, Robert was his father's son. And if Grace was sure of anything it was of her stepfather's love.

Adrian whipped round to confront his brother. "You keep out of this. She's got to learn her place. *We're* father's true sons. She isn't even related to us."

"Grace lost her mother and father. She doesn't have anyone else but us."

Adrian's scowl turned into a cruel smile as he turned back to his stepsister. "Then, brother, she has no family. There, I've solved the problem. Out she goes. I'll talk to father."

Robert's eyes became round and his mouth opened into a large 'O'. "But where would she go?"

Adrian shrugged his shoulders and that horrible smile remained. It chilled Grace's blood.

"Who knows? She can live on the streets for all I care. She can perish in the winter storms, drown herself in the sea, throw herself off a cliff. Who would even miss her?"

Tears stung Grace's eyes, but she mustn't give way to them. Then he would have won, and she knew from past experience that a victorious Adrian was even more offensive than a defeated one. She bit her lip and said nothing, but lowered her gaze once more to her boots and prayed for the day to end.

After tea, she fled to the sanctuary of her room and shut the door firmly behind her. This was the one place in this hated house that she could escape from her stepbrother's sarcasm, taunts and bullying. Grace threw herself on her bed and burst into tears. She clutched the counterpane in her fists and sobbed for her dead mother. For her own loneliness. Her small hand tightened around the silver locket she always wore around her neck.

"Mama, why did you have to leave me?" No one answered.

If only I could grow up fast, she thought. *I could leave here, become a governess or a nanny and I would never have to see Adrian again.*

Gradually, her tears dried and her sobs subsided, but still she lay there, in the peace and tranquility of her room. The sun set, casting orange flames through the window onto the carpet. Grace watched them fade as she sprawled on the bed, her hair falling around her shoulders.

Shadows lengthened and a full moon rose, its silvery beams replacing the sun's golden rays. Outside, she heard the hoot of an owl and imagined it flying overhead, alert for any sign of movement on the ground. How she longed to be able to open her window and fly off into the distance, without a care. She envied birds their freedom.

If only…

Finally, she sat up and leaned over to unbutton her boots, flexing her toes as she removed each one. Then she unfastened her skirt and blouse and slipped into her nightgown, before she fastened her robe around her and lit her candle. Then followed a short trip to the lavatory, scurrying up and down the corridor as fast as she could, without extinguishing the flickering flame. She took special care to tread lightly past Adrian's closed door.

Back in bed, she removed her locket for her nightly ritual. She opened it and gazed down at the photographs. On the left-hand side, her parents on their wedding day. Her mother was seated and her father stood behind, a protective hand on her shoulder. Both stared straight at the camera, unsmiling and dignified. The photo on the right showed her mother alone. Taken from her left side, her hands were clasped in her lap, her hair tied firmly back in a bun; the same locket Grace held hung around her neck. Only then, it would have contained a photo of Grace.

"God bless Mama, God bless Papa." Grace placed a light kiss on both photos as she did every night. Then she fastened the locket back around her neck, snuffed out the candle and lay back against the cool, clean pillow. It smelled comfortingly of sunshine and crisp island air. Grace turned on her right side and let her mind drift.

Oh, why was Adrian so horrible to her? She only wanted a word of approval from him. Was she really such a terrible person that he could feel so threatened by her? What had she ever done to deserve such treatment? Tears started at the back of her eyes and she tossed aside the bedclothes. On bare feet, she padded over to the tall chest on the far side of her room and tugged open the deep bottom drawer. She rummaged in the dark for a few moments before her hand touched something cold. Lydia, her doll. Papa had brought her back from Edinburgh, where it seemed he had contracted the illness that killed him.

Grace pulled the doll out of the drawer and hugged her close. Then she took her to the window to look at her. The serene, porcelain face smiled up at her through rosy lips. Her hair was neatly coiffed and her sensible, governess-like dress, with its long sleeves and modest neckline, reminded her a little of Mama.

Fresh tears trickled down Grace's cheeks and splashed onto the doll's pretty face. The pain of her mother's loss gnawed relentlessly at her stomach, even two years on. No matter how much Stepfather tried, he was not a naturally affectionate father. She couldn't sit on his knee and be cuddled as her own father would have done. But then, as an only child, she had enjoyed Papa's sole attention.

Jonas had the two boys and behaved just as distantly with them. Oh, she had no doubt he loved them, but their father locked himself away in his study with his collections, only emerging at mealtimes and to say "good night". Just like her, the boys were growing up parentless, their care entrusted to a strict, but fair, tutor from Aberdeen called Mr. Angus—nicknamed "Bull" by Adrian. Grace thought it a silly nickname. With his ginger hair, Mr. Angus looked nothing like the majestic black cattle in Mr. McMurtry's fields.

———————

The following morning, Grace joined the boys in the schoolroom. She shot a quick glance at Adrian who was already seated at his desk. He ignored her. Robert's brief smile disappeared in a flash as Adrian glanced over and scowled. Grace knew that, even though Robert tried to stick up for her, he was just as much afraid of his elder brother as she was.

She opened her exercise book and chewed the end of her pencil, hoping she could remember the lines of the poem Mr. Angus had instructed her to memorize. She had known it the day before, but then had been too upset to practice it again during the evening. Oh well, too late now.

The door creaked a little as Mr. Angus threw it open and strode in, a pile of books under his arm and a grim expression on his face. His unruly thatch of ginger hair badly needed a trim and his moustache grew bushy and untamed, submerging his top lip. He slammed the books down on his desk and faced his pupils.

As always, Grace sat in front, while the boys' desks were positioned around four feet apart behind her to form a triangle. This gave their tutor the advantage of being able to ensure no one cheated and to move unhindered among them, checking on their progress.

"Good morning, class," he said, as always.

"Good morning, Mr. Angus," they said in unison.

"I have read your essays and, as usual, only one passed muster. I will discuss the merits and demerits of each one later. For now though,

I wish to find out if you have memorized your part of Lord Tennyson's excellent poem, 'The Charge of the Light Brigade'. I will listen to you recite it first and then we will discuss the history of the time the poet was writing about. Adrian, you will start us off please."

Grace heard the shuffling of feet behind her and held her breath. Silence.

"Come along, Adrian. We're all waiting for you."

More shuffling of feet, this time accompanied by a slight cough.

"Adrian, do I really have to tell you again?"

"No, sir."

"Then get on with it, boy!"

"'Half a…mile—"

Mr. Angus's hands crashed down on the desk, toppling books onto the floor. Grace jumped.

"How *dare* you, boy! Seventeen years old and you can't even learn a few lines of one of the best known poems by one of our best loved poets. Dammit, I knew the words to this poem when I was six years old! Are you stupid or just plain lazy? Come on, boy! Answer me! Which is it?"

"Neither, sir."

"*Neither?*" Foam bubbled from the corners of the tutor's mouth.

Grace had never seen him so angry. She flinched. The movement attracted Mr. Angus's attention, but when he spoke to her, his voice was much softer.

"Now then, Grace. I don't expect you will let me down. Have you learned the poem?"

She could only manage a shy squeak. "Yes, sir."

"Then please begin."

Grace coughed. Her mouth dried and she found it difficult to speak. She opened her mouth, closed it and then, aware that Mr. Angus's frown had reappeared, opened it again. Hesitant at first, she gained confidence and her voice grew stronger as the words flooded back to her.

"'*Half a league, half a league,*
Half a league onward,
All in the valley of Death,

Rode the six hundred.
"Forward, the Light Brigade!
Charge for the guns!" he said:
Into the valley of Death
Rode the six hundred."'

Grace paused and wondered if he wanted her to continue. The words of the second verse flooded into her mind and she could carry on, but she could feel Adrian's eyes burning into the back of her head and her spirits sank. He would make her pay for this later.

"Thank you, Grace. I am gratified to see that at least one member of this class takes her studies seriously."

Robert made no sound and Grace wondered what was going through his young head. In a normal household, Adrian wouldn't have been schooled at home like this, but his mother made Jonas promise he would never send him away to boarding school and there could be no question of a boy of his class attending the local school here on the island. In this matter, as in so many fatherly duties, Jonas had found the problems it caused too difficult and time-consuming, so he preferred to ignore them. He hired Mr. Angus and gave the tutor a free hand to try and teach all three children as much as they were capable of learning. Then he shut the door of his study and busied himself with his collections.

Grace loved acquiring knowledge. Learning came easily to her and memorizing verse upon verse of poetry presented no trial at all.

Mr. Angus hadn't finished with her stepbrother yet. "Adrian, as punishment for your disobedience, you will learn the next two verses of that poem and be ready to recite them tomorrow morning at nine sharp. Do you understand?"

"Yes, sir."

Grace could almost hear the scowl that must now be pasted across his face and shivered.

The class moved on to a discussion of their essays. The theme had been birds. Robert read out a childish, but quite charming, account of guillemots flying over the nearby lake in autumn and received a silver star for his efforts. The gold star was, as usual, awarded to Grace for an essay about an arctic tern, all alone and swimming across the lake on a cold, gray, misty day. She saw Mr. Angus brush away a tear as she described how a hungry skua had swooped out of the sky and scooped the little tern up out of the lake. Grace had used some poetic license here, as she wasn't even sure a skua would attack terns. But it made for a good story and Mr. Angus, hailing from the big city of Aberdeen, probably wouldn't know anyway.

When she had finished, the tutor applauded. "That was utterly charming, Grace. Well done. One day, if you carry on like this, I will be reading your stories in The Strand magazine."

Grace's pride swelled and she beamed. Who cared about horrid Adrian? Mr. Angus thought her good enough for the same magazine that published those wonderful stories by Mr. Conan Doyle that she pored over whenever her stepfather had finished with his copy. She couldn't wait to read the latest exploits of his wonderful detective, Sherlock Holmes, and his assistant, Dr. Watson.

Mr. Angus's smile faded as he switched his attention to Adrian. The tutor picked up a sheet of paper and, even though she sat some feet away, Grace could see the blotches of ink staining the creamy, lined sheet.

"As always, at the opposite end of the scale from Grace's moving and most excellent essay, we have this sloppy, blotched effort, consisting of just one sheet of paper, from Adrian." The tutor sighed.

"I won't bother to hand it back to you and I certainly won't sully my ears or those of your brother and stepsister by having you read it out. The spelling is appalling, the grammar is, if anything, worse. You write like a six-year-old who has never set eyes on a bird, much less written about one. It's Wednesday today. You have until Friday to produce an acceptable essay, consisting of no fewer than three pages. To start with, after class this afternoon, you can take yourself down to the lake with a notebook and watch the birds. Take note of what they are doing. Select your subject and be back here for seven p.m., when I shall be here to supervise your detention."

"But, sir—"

Adrian's protest was ill-conceived. Mr. Angus's temper, when riled, could prove as fiery as his hair.

"No buts!" His voice rang around the room and echoed off the walls. Grace squeezed her eyes shut and then opened them again.

Adrian didn't protest again and the lesson moved on to a discussion of the Battle of Balaclava during the Crimean War and why it had so inspired Lord Tennyson.

When class finished for the day, Mr. Angus asked Grace to stay behind.

Adrian scowled at her as he left the room.

"Don't forget," Mr. Angus said to him, "seven o'clock sharp. Back here with your notes. And any more of those looks and you'll find yourself in detention every evening this week."

Robert slipped past Grace and gave her a reassuring smile. Grace returned it, grateful that at least *he* wasn't angry with her.

"Shut the door please, Grace, I have something I want to tell you."

Grace stood, crossed to the door and latched it firmly. Then she returned to her desk and sat down.

Mr. Angus leaned forward and rested his elbows on the desk.

"Grace, I count it a privilege to teach you. You are always attentive in class, always complete your assignments and produce work of a consistently high standard. You are to be commended."

Grace stared, feeling overcome. No one had ever complimented her like that. "Thank you, sir."

He waved his hand. "Not at all. You deserve to be praised for the effort you put in, unlike one of your stepbrothers. He really shouldn't be in this class at all. The boy is seventeen years old for goodness' sake."

He seemed about to say more, but corrected himself. No doubt he realized, just in time, that he had no place criticizing his employer's son. Especially not to the boy's despised stepsister.

Grace continued to stare at him and wondered what was coming next. From his expression, the tutor seemed to be having a battle with himself. Then he gave the merest of nods, as if he had made a decision at last.

"Grace, what I am about to say is said with the utmost respect. First, I need to ask you a question. Are you afraid of Adrian?"

Grace jumped. She hadn't been prepared for that. Her feelings about her stepbrother were matters only for her and not to be discussed. Only once had she voiced them to her mother who had told her to stop being such a ninny and make an effort to get on with him. She had made it quite clear she didn't expect to hear any whining like that ever again. So Grace had done her best to get along with a boy who clearly resented her existence. When all attempts had failed, she turned to her doll, Lydia, whose calm face always soothed away her tears.

"I'm sorry, Grace, I didn't mean to startle you, but I need to know the truth. Does Adrian bully you?"

She wanted to tell him, to confess she cried herself to sleep night after night at the unfairness of it all, that her fears turned to nightmares that woke her in the night, quaking and frightened to close her eyes. But Mama had said "no".

But then, Mama wasn't here anymore, was she? Could she hear her from heaven?

Grace touched her locket, took a deep breath and opened her mouth.

"No, sir." Even *she* couldn't believe she had just said that, but the conditioning was just too strong. Besides, Mama might just be able to hear her and would surely punish her from beyond the grave if she dared confess such a personal family truth to an outsider.

Mr. Angus's eyebrows met the lock of hair straggling across his forehead. "Are you sure? You can tell me in confidence and I promise I will tell no one else."

Grace blinked hard. Such a tempting offer. What a relief it would be to say "yes" and have someone else share the burden. A voice inside her head built to a crescendo. It demanded she tell him the truth. She didn't know what he could do, but maybe Mr. Angus could talk to Stepfather. Maybe *he* could then give Adrian a good dressing down and force the boy to stop bullying her.

But Mama had said "no".

Grace lowered her eyes and shook her head.

Mr. Angus leaned back and sighed.

"Of course, I am aware I cannot force you to tell me, but I believe the reason for your denial is that he has frightened you so much you daren't speak out. Grace, no human being has the right to exercise so much control over another human being. Do you understand?"

She didn't really, but she nodded anyway. It all sounded like fine words. Easy to say when you weren't the victim.

"Grace, look at me when I'm speaking to you."

With an effort, Grace raised her eyes to his and noticed for the first time how green they were.

"I want you to be very careful of that stepbrother of yours. I believe he can be very dangerous and could commit serious harm to anyone who crosses him. I want you to promise me you'll never be anywhere alone with him. When you have to be in his company, make sure there is always a responsible adult— your stepfather, me or the housekeeper—with you as well. If no one is around, make sure you leave the room. You can make up an excuse. Say you have to collect something you've forgotten from your room. Can you lock your door?"

A wave of panic hit Grace. He would surely never go into her room. Why would she need to lock the door?

"I can see that disturbs you, but if you have a key, use it. Best to be safe than sorry. Adrian is an extraordinarily vindictive and resentful young man. He is so full of hatred, it clouds his judgment and, with a person like that, it is far safer to keep well away. They can be like a cornered tiger and I've seen one of those in India. Believe me, you don't want to be anywhere near when that animal attacks—and it will. Mark my words. Now, I will ask again, is there anything you want to tell me about Adrian?"

Tell him! Tell him! Grace's mind screamed. But again she lowered her eyes and shook her head. This time, she clasped her hands tightly even though she knew he was watching and didn't believe a word of her denial.

Mr. Angus sighed again. More deeply this time. "Very well, Grace, you may go. But please remember my words and be careful. Will you promise me?"

Grace stood, glad to be able to escape. She rewarded Mr. Angus with the briefest of nods and most fleeting of smiles before dashing from the room, straight to her own bedroom.

Once inside, she leaned against the door, then reached behind her and found the key. She turned it and, for the first time in her life, locked herself in her bedroom.

She saw something out of the corner of her eye. On the bed, Lydia lay where she had left her this morning. She'd decided not to return the doll to her drawer; Lydia could lie on a soft counterpane for a change. A reward for being her faithful companion all these years, and for being the only thing she had left of her father.

But, as she looked down at the mangled mess in front of her, she let out a wail. Someone had smashed the doll's face and it lay shattered into tiny shards. They'd ripped her dress and then stuck a giant hatpin through her chest, just where her heart would be if she had been human.

If she had been Grace herself.

Grace clutched the ruined doll to her chest and howled with pain. She didn't care if anyone heard her—not even the perpetrator of this dreadful crime. And she knew who it was. Who it could only be. Mr. Angus was right. Adrian hated her and he would stop at nothing to hurt her.

Chapter Four

I had the falling dream. You know, the one that catches you when you're in that semi-conscious state between wakefulness and sleep. It's sudden, dramatic and lasts barely a second, but in that instant, you experience the terror of being thrown off a precipice into a bottomless pit. Most of the time, you just shudder and then drop off to sleep. This one shook me awake.

Beside me, Greg slept on, oblivious. I wished I could sleep like him. No matter what was on his mind, he could just drop off wherever and whenever he chose.

Fully awake now, I sat up and moved as gently as possible. The room was quiet and still, but it felt wrong. The old familiar chill passed through me.

I caught my breath. A faint glow misted in the far corner of the room, swirled and then shimmered as it transformed into the recognizable shape of a woman. I hadn't imagined it at the lake; she really had followed me here. My specter.

Her hollow eyes stared out at me. Could she see or just feel my presence?

The black hole, where her mouth should be, grew rounder, as if she had opened it to speak, but, as always, no words drifted towards me. So far, all had been as before, except for the surprise of seeing her here. What happened next was different.

From her mouth, a foggy white vapor curled. It writhed and twisted and, to my horror, wafted towards me. I shrank back against the headboard and drew my knees up to my chin. Should I wake Greg? If he saw it, he would have to believe me now.

I shook his shoulder. He groaned a little.

"Greg!" My dry mouth produced more of a furious whisper than a cry.

Still he slept.

I shook him so hard, the bed quaked. No reaction. Surely no one could have slept through that. The specter must have done something to make him sleep on. Unless I was dreaming.

If only.

As the vapor drew nearer, I heard voices in my head. I couldn't make out what they were saying. Too many, all speaking at once. Chattering whispers, growing louder. Urgent. Imploring. Warning. Somewhere in there, I could make out just one word. A name.

Grace.

My heart thumped and joined the cacophony in my head. I clapped my hands to my ears, as if that would stem the noise or rid my brain of the endless din. Then, one second I was in physical pain from the roar and the next, it echoed and faded into the distance.

I realized I'd squeezed my eyes shut and now opened them. My gaze shot to where my specter had stood, but the corner was empty. I switched on the bedside lamp and lowered my feet to the floor. In the bathroom, the glass clattered against the porcelain when I filled it with cold water. Then, as I drank, I caught sight of myself in the bathroom mirror. My skin was parchment white, as if all the blood had drained away. My eyes were big, wide, still unnerved by my experience.

I switched off the light, padded back to bed and tucked the duvet around me. I found it mildly comforting to be cocooned in its softness. Greg's peaceful, rhythmical breathing was the only sound as I tried to make sense of what had just happened. I also decided not to breathe a word of it to Greg. Not only because he wouldn't believe me but also because, for whatever reason, my specter didn't want him to know.

The strongest feeling of danger enveloped me. It found a home there that night and never left.

Still the rain pelted down but still it didn't matter, although poor Laurence seemed to think he held a personal responsibility for the elements and their potential to ruin our holiday.

"Och, it's such a shame. And you've come all this way too. I am so sorry you're not having better weather. It was so lovely and warm up until the day you arrived."

"Yes, it *is* a shame," I said. "But we might as well make the best of it. I'm finding the museum really interesting and the curator is so helpful. I'm getting lots of information for my book."

Greg smiled. "And I'm keeping up to date with my work as well as taking a little time off to relax, so there's really no harm done."

Laurence looked from one to the other of us. "Well, I suppose that's all right then. Just as long as you're both enjoying yourselves."

"Oh, yes, indeed," I said and wished I was telling the whole truth.

Laurence trotted off back to the kitchen and we finished our breakfast.

"Seriously, are you going back to the museum today?" Greg asked.

A sudden twinge stabbed me. Did Greg want to go sightseeing? In the *rain*?

"I was planning to, but did you have something else in mind?"

"No, that's fine. I'm just concerned that you must be very bored. The trouble is you need good weather on this island. You need to be able to walk, without splashing around in rain and mud."

I dabbed my mouth with my napkin and set it down on the table. "I'm really enjoying my research. The more I learn about Jonas Devine and his dysfunctional family, the more I want to know, and Duncan is so helpful and knowledgeable."

Greg smiled. "Just as long as that's all he is."

I threw the napkin at him. "Get away with you."

Greg laughed.

———

"Well, hello again. Can't stay away I see."

Duncan's welcoming smile made me feel as if we had known each other for years. I found it comforting, until I remembered the secret I had hidden in the wardrobe. With an effort, I pushed aside the guilt.

Until I knew why I had stolen it, I daren't allow myself to dwell too much.

"There's nothing on the internet, but I'd like to find out more about Adrian Devine."

The smile died on Duncan's face.

"I'm afraid that's going to be difficult."

Duncan moved around to my side of the counter and beckoned me to the seats. When we had sat down, he continued, "Tradition has it that, after Grace drowned, Robert—the younger son—raced back to the house and told his father what had happened. It seems the boy left nothing out. That meant when Adrian wandered in some time later, smelling of drink from the alehouse, his father's fury had reached boiling point. He told him he no longer regarded him as his son and ordered him to leave, right then and there. Adrian protested his innocence of course, but Robert wouldn't budge from his story. He stood up to his bullying older brother for the first and only time in his life, because two days later, Adrian was on a boat for the mainland with a couple of hundred pounds in his pocket and a one-way ticket. He was never heard from again."

Now what would I do? With Adrian disappeared, the trail had grown cold.

"Didn't he even write home?"

Duncan shook his head. "If he did, the letters were destroyed. Jonas wouldn't allow his name mentioned in the house. He really loved Grace, you see, and he never fully recovered from her death, or, more particularly, the *manner* in which she died. I can't imagine how he must have felt. His beloved stepdaughter, left to drown like that by his own flesh and blood."

I shuddered. "Adrian Devine must have been a thoroughly nasty piece of work. It wouldn't surprise me if he continued to behave like that wherever he ended up. He sounds like some kind of sociopath."

Duncan nodded. "I had the same experience as you when I searched for him on the internet, so you might try the Scottish General Records Office. I keep meaning to do it. I just never seem to get around to it. They have a website and you could request a search. It's a simple enough procedure although I understand they do make an administrative charge. From memory, I think you already know the information you'll need to complete their form."

"As long as it doesn't break the bank, I might just do that. One more thing; whatever happened to the other son, Robert? The trauma of that day must have stayed with him a long time. Maybe even scarred him for life."

Duncan smiled. "Aye. But he managed to put it largely behind him in the end. The years went by and he left the island to read Medicine at the university in Edinburgh. There, he met a lovely girl called Stella Jardine and they were married in 1915, just before Robert went off to serve in France during the First World War. Thankfully, he survived almost being blown up when a bomb exploded nearby. It left him with permanent tinnitus but otherwise unscathed."

"Did he ever return to Arnsay? His father must have missed him."

"I'm sure he did but, sadly, Jonas died in 1916 while his son was serving in France. He caught a chill that worsened into bronchitis and then pneumonia. He left the house to Robert, who couldn't bear the thought of living in it, so he bequeathed it, and all its contents, to the people of Arnsay. I think his father would have approved and even been proud of him for it."

As I listened to Duncan, I had the oddest impression that he had more than an academic interest in the fate of Robert Devine.

"You sound as if you knew him."

He smiled. "I didn't fully answer your previous question, did I? Robert trained as a doctor and returned to the island, in 1936, with his wife and ten-year-old daughter, also named Grace. He became the local GP and remained here until his death in 1978 at the ripe old age of eighty-six. He was my grandfather."

I must have stared at him open-mouthed for a second, because he burst out laughing. "If I had a camera now, I'd photograph your face!"

I snapped my mouth shut. "I had no idea that was coming!" I said. "So you're Adrian Devine's…great-nephew? Is that right?"

"Right."

"So that's how you know he never contacted anyone."

"I can't see that he could have. Unless he tried to persuade his father to change his mind, in the early days. I truly believe if Jonas

Devine had received any communication from his eldest son, he would have destroyed it. Probably unopened. My grandfather told me he was unwavering in his determination to disown him. Even wrote him out of his will. Everything went to Robert."

"And Robert never lived here after his father died?"

"Only for a few nights. He managed to obtain compassionate leave to attend his father's funeral and make necessary arrangements for disposal of his estate. He told me he found the house eerie, especially upstairs where the collection is housed now. Are you all right?"

I nodded, but the chill that crept up from my stomach told another story. As did the now familiar goosebumps rising on my arms. "How long have you been curator here?"

"Oh, around fifteen years, I suppose."

"And have you ever felt anything…odd?"

He stared at me for a long moment before responding. "By odd, what do you mean exactly?"

"Upstairs. Whispers, shadows moving, that sort of thing. Things you can't rationally explain?"

He inhaled. "Sometimes. Let's say, I prefer to go up there when someone else is around. We have had cleaners who have lasted a week and then left because they didn't like the feeling of being constantly watched. They didn't mean the CCTV either."

He pointed up at a camera. Of course!

"Do you monitor the CCTV at all? I mean, when people say they've experienced something strange, do you check the date and time and play back the recording?"

Duncan shifted awkwardly in his seat. I'd hit a nerve.

"I used to."

"And have you seen anything?"

"Sometimes."

Why was he being so cagey? "Could you show me?" I smiled in what I hoped was an encouraging fashion.

He shook his head. "No."

"May I ask why not?"

He sighed and ran his fingers through his hair. "Because, most likely, you'll see nothing at all. I know it sounds impossible, but whenever I've played back the recording, the…entity…has appeared once, but when I rewind, it's gone again. There's nothing but normal footage of an empty room, or one with the affected person reacting, apparently, to nothing."

"But that's impossible, surely? I mean, it's either on the recording or not. It can't be there one time and gone the next."

"You tell the …whatever it is up there…that."

Duncan's normally affable features were history and, in front of me, stood a scared and troubled man.

"Duncan, why do you stay here if it frightens you so much?"

He looked at me, sadness in his brown eyes. "I enjoy my job, and I feel I owe it to my grandfather. Then there's Grace's memory. Besides, whatever it is usually stays in one place and, as long as I steer clear of it, there's no problem. I've never thought it was particularly interested in me anyway. It seems to be searching for something. I can't really explain it, and it's probably just my fancy, anyway."

"When I was upstairs, I felt it. I may have even heard it."

Duncan blinked rapidly. "You too? I wondered why you were asking all the questions."

"Have you ever seen her? Grace, I mean. Perhaps down by the lakeside?"

Duncan shook his head. "No, but I've heard others who claim they have. She stands there, in a white floral dress, holding her new hat and staring out over the lake where she drowned. I don't know why she would only have worn a white floral dress though. It was a bitterly cold January day. Surely, she would have worn her coat…" His voice faded and, for a moment, I thought he was going to burst into tears. But, the moment passed and he recovered himself.

"When you've seen these images on the playback, what has the apparition looked like?"

He screwed up his face. "Nothing I could accurately describe. Not human. Not like any animal I've ever seen either. It's just a shape, and it changes, sort of swirls, a bit like a mist, but it has substance. It seems to drape itself around the person it's affecting, rather like a shawl. As the person moves, so does the thing around them. Then, at some point, they run out of the gallery and the entity loosens itself and disappears."

"You mean it evaporates?"

"Not always. Sometimes, it sinks to the floor and scurries away. Like a rat. Out of camera shot."

I put my hand to my mouth. "Oh, God, Duncan, did you see the footage of me in the gallery?" For a heart stopping moment, I realized that if he had, he almost certainly would have seen me steal the picture.

"No, I've switched the cameras off up there. Did it about a month ago. Frankly, I just couldn't handle the stress. As far as I'm concerned, out of sight is out of mind. I only know I don't want to see that thing again, When I know I won't be able to prove it later, I'd rather not see it at all."

I breathed an inward sigh of relief. Somehow, probably very soon, I would have to return that picture and I couldn't bring myself to confess and hand it over. Duncan would be so disappointed in me and never trust me again. I was sure of that. But the prospect of climbing those stairs and going into that gallery alone again sent yet more shivers racing up and down my spine.

I struggled to find alternatives. Hang on to the picture? Take it home? Throw it in the nearest garbage bin? All possibilities. Why on earth had I put myself in this predicament?

Some irresistible urge had made me steal it in the first place. And I knew I would have to let it reveal its secrets, however scared that might make me.

Chapter Five

"It's not altogether surprising they're related," Greg said as we lingered over our after-dinner coffee in the hotel. "What's the island population? Around five thousand? I don't think it's grown much, if at all, in the last hundred years. Probably declined if anything."

"True." I had a sudden urge to talk about something else. "What do you fancy doing tonight? Strolling by the lake? Drinks in the bar here or the pub up the road?"

Greg thought for a moment. "A little stroll up to the pub, couple of drinks and an early night. How does that sound?"

"Great. I'll get my jacket."

"I'll wait at reception."

In our room, a dripping noise came from the bathroom. I must have left a tap running, so I pushed the door open…and stared.

The bath had overflowed with greenish water. Incredibly, small blocks of ice floated on the surface. I put one reluctant foot in front of the other, crossed the room and leaned over.

She lay on the bottom, her eyes closed. Grace Devine in her white floral dress with her locket around her neck. I froze. This couldn't be… She couldn't be…

Her eyes snapped open. I screamed.

Her long, white arm reached out to me and I blacked out.

Greg found me on the bathroom floor. "Alex. Oh, thank God. What on earth happened?"

My head buzzed and it took a moment to realize where I was. Greg cradled me in his arms as he sat on the bone-dry floor.

I wrenched myself free, struggled to my feet and saw the bath — empty and as dry as the floor. No sign of Grace or the mess I had discovered.

"How long was I out? Was the room like this when you got here?"

Greg stood and stared at me with a bemused expression. "I came to find you after about five minutes and, yes, of course the room was like this. How else would it have been?"

Should I tell him? But I knew how he would react and I wasn't up for it right then. I shook my head. "I'm not quite myself yet. Just ignore me."

I could tell Greg wasn't convinced. "Did you slip and bang your head or something? Do you need to see a doctor?"

The buzzing had stopped and my head felt less muzzy. "No, I'm fine now. Maybe I had a sudden drop in blood sugar or something. Let's go for that walk."

"Oh no, you don't. You're going to lie down and rest."

"But it's only nine o'clock and I'm fine now."

"Alex. You fainted. There has to be a reason for that and if it happens once more, you're seeing the doctor, whether you like it or not."

Rarely had I ever heard Greg use that dictatorial tone with me. We didn't have that sort of marriage. In my vows, I had never promised to obey and I certainly wasn't about to start now, but he did have a point. I had no explanation for what had happened in the bathroom. Did I imagine it? Or was it yet another example of the psychic ability that let me see Grace and my specter, and a few other things most people seemed not to capture? Whatever the reason, I wished it would all stop and leave me alone.

In that instant, I had the strongest urge to leave Arnsay and never return. But how would I explain *that* to Greg? Too exhausted to think straight, I had to say something. Greg wouldn't give up until I had answered him. "I think you're right. I do feel like slipping into that bed and going to sleep."

"At last, a bit of common sense. I thought I was in for an argument there. An early night will do us both good. Then we'll see how you feel in the morning."

I overslept and woke to find Greg tapping away at his laptop. I ran my fingers through my tousled hair and tried to focus. "What time is it?"

"Ah, there you are. It's eight thirty-five. I let you sleep, because you obviously needed it. How do you feel this morning?"

How did I feel? Surprisingly well, for someone who had come upon a ghost in a flooded bathroom only to faint and then discover she had imagined it all. Well, probably. I yawned. "I'm ready to get up and get on with the day." I stood up and stretched.

"You'll be amazed to learn that it's stopped raining, so if you want to do some sightseeing, I suggest we go out straight after breakfast."

"Great," I said and tried to sound more enthusiastic than I felt.

An hour later, we were dressed in sensible boots, waterproof jackets and my trusty Barbour hat was thrust into my pocket. I'd decided to leave my handbag at home for once and had tucked it away in the room safe. I needed both hands free if we were going to go scrambling over rocks.

"I thought we'd look at that stone circle," Greg said. "It's about half an hour's walk away according to Laurence. The ground's probably sodden but we're dressed for it so we should be okay."

I nodded. Despite my ambivalent feelings towards the island, I couldn't help a twinge of excitement. All my life, I'd been a pushover for prehistoric monuments, megaliths, stone circles and anything ancient and mysterious. Stonehenge, Callanish and Skara Brae sent me into raptures.

In my left pocket, I carried our little camera and fully intended to get some shots of the Arnsay Circle.

The sunshine had brought out hikers and birds of all breeds. The puffy white clouds provided a stark contrast to the vivid blue sky and I hadn't hiked more than a hundred yards before I unzipped my jacket.

Greg did likewise. "It's so much warmer today."

"We'd better make the most of it. This is probably the only summer we're going to get." I inhaled the clear, warm air with its overtones of fresh, dewy grass and tinges of lilac—an impressive example of which we were fast approaching.

"Gorgeous smell," Greg said as he twitched his nose.

"Isn't it? Always reminds me of my grandmother. Mum's mother. She had an old-fashioned garden with lilacs, honeysuckle and hollyhocks, oh, and those strange red and yellow flowers we called red hot pokers."

"Oh, yes. I'd forgotten them. Did she have a monkey puzzle tree by any chance? My Nan did."

"No, I think I would have remembered that."

We rounded a corner and Greg pointed over at a field on our left.

"Look. Over there. I'm sure that's it."

The closer we got, the clearer it became: a collection of standing stones, each six or seven feet high. We stopped by a gate and read the brown sign. 'Arnsay Circle, ancient monument.'

"Camera ready?"

I nodded. We trudged over the long grass and my jeans soon became streaked with rain and dew. In the exposed field, the breeze brought a distinct chill, so I zipped up my jacket again and carried on.

Greg stood a little way ahead of me and I paused to take his photograph. "Greg!"

He turned and I clicked the shutter.

He laughed. "You always do that and I always fall for it. My hair was over my eyes and there's probably a megalith growing out of my head. If you post that on the internet, I'll sue!"

I laughed and checked the picture. It looked okay, although there seemed to be a bit of camera flash in the top left corner just above Greg's head. Strange because I hadn't been aware of the flash going off.

"Come on, Alex. Come and see this Viking graffiti."

I switched off the camera and ran towards him.

The circle comprised twelve standing stones, with a further eight or nine fallen, broken and scattered around the nearby landscape. Greg peered at some symbols etched into the surface of one of the erect stones.

I recognized the shapes. Viking runes. I hoped the nearby information board would provide a translation, and it did. "It says here that the inscription concerns the merits of some woman called Gunnild. Evidently she must have pleased the man who carved these runes as he describes her as having wondrous long hair and a generous body. Randy little sod, wasn't he?"

"Viking trait, I think. There's something similar on the wall at Maeshowe in Orkney, don't you remember?"

"I was just thinking about that. You don't suppose it was the same guy, do you?"

"Who knows? It wouldn't be impossible. Do you want to get some more shots? But please, leave me out of them. I hate posing."

"Then don't. I'll just catch you au naturel."

"Er—not in this wind you won't."

I snapped away at the stones, and, every now and again, snapped Greg when he wasn't looking.

"Okay, now it's my turn." He reached for the camera and I handed it over. "Now you go and have a proper look round them. I'll look after this for you."

He grinned and I knew he'd sneak in some shots of me. I'd look windswept and disheveled and, as soon as I could, I'd delete them. I always did.

Ten minutes later, we were ready to head off somewhere else.

"There's a chambered tomb a little farther up the road," Greg said. "Laurence told me there's a sign. It's called Ansgar's Tomb, probably named after some Viking who discovered it. It's even older than the stone circle. About 3600 BC. Apparently it just looks like a grassy mound from the road, but you can actually walk into it, as long as you bend down for the first few feet. Then it opens up. They found around twenty skeletons there in the 1930s."

"Sounds like Maeshowe again."

"The way Laurence described it, it sounded like a cross between that and West Kennet down in Wiltshire."

"Should be interesting."

It was. And it also frightened me half to death.

The familiar brown sign pointed us in the right direction and we strode up the stony path, half a mile or so towards the grassy mound. As we approached it, we could see the stone archway. We had to bend almost double to clamber inside and the entrance formed a narrow tunnel, with massive stone slabs either side. Fortunately, the archaeologists hadn't entirely covered the roof in grass, to allow natural light to filter in through some kind of Perspex. When the tunnel opened up into a large open space, we could see chambers on either side, separated by more massive slabs, each of which must have weighed many tons. The main tomb itself extended maybe ninety feet in a rectangle, with a width of, perhaps, a third of that, but the chambers opened up into separate rooms, so the whole project must have been a massive undertaking, both for the original builders and the archaeologists who discovered it.

I wandered into one of the chambers on my own, while Greg went deeper inside. I could hear his footsteps as they crunched the gravel floor of the tomb and then faded into the distance. No one else was around and I perched on a low stone, to soak up the atmosphere.

I had been there maybe two minutes.

"Get out of here!"

The unfamiliar female voice startled me. I sprang to my feet. No one there. "Greg?" My voice bounced off the walls.

From far away, I heard him. "Yes? What is it?"

I darted out into the main tomb and gazed around. No one there.

"Leave. Now!"

I spun around, certain the voice came from behind me. Again, no one.

"Greg, I've got to get out of here. Now."

He appeared from one of the small chambers at the far end. I turned and bent down to get through the tunnel and hoped against hope I didn't run into whoever—whatever— had threatened me. Tears streamed down my face and I was trembling, stumbling. Someone breathed close behind me. *Oh God, let me get out of here alive!*

I emerged into the sunlight, coughing and choking back sobs. I screamed as arms went around me, only to realize they were Greg's. It must have been his breathing I heard.

He clasped me to him, his face serious. Then he released me and held me at arm's length.

"What on earth was all that about?"

Oh, what the hell. I couldn't keep it to myself. "While I was in the small chamber on my own, a voice spoke to me. It told me to get out. That's when I called to you. Then it happened again. In the main tomb." A fresh wave of sobs.

Greg handed me a tissue, but said nothing. He probably hadn't a clue what to do with me at that moment.

My earlier shock drained away, but anger welled up in its place. "You know, Greg, sometimes there just isn't a rational explanation. Sometimes there really *are* forces at work we don't understand."

"Not in my world."

"Yes, in your world too. You're just too stubborn to accept it." We stared at each other for a few moments, our lovely day ruined.

"I vote we go back now," Greg said at last. "I'm not in the mood for any more history today."

"We can agree on that, at least." I thrust my hands into my pockets and my fingers closed around the camera. I'd upload the photos on to Greg's laptop when we got back to the hotel. It might take my mind off disembodied voices and Greg's bullheadedness.

But Greg uploaded the pictures, so he saw the anomaly first.

"You need to clean the camera lens. Every one of these pictures has some kind of white mark on them."

"Eh? I cleaned it this morning, before we went out. I used the lens cloth too, so there wouldn't be any smears."

"Come and see for yourself."

He stood to let me sit on the chair by the desk.

The first picture I had taken filled the screen. Sure enough, the anomaly I had thought of as camera flash wafted like mist, over Greg's head. Using the program controls, I isolated the appropriate segment and enlarged it to the point where it was starting to break up. Then I took it down a few percentage points and peered at it closely.

"It's a shape. Maybe a woman."

Greg leaned over my shoulder. "What? Oh, come on, Alex. You sound like one of those lunatics that finds Jesus in a potato."

I ignored him as anger crept up inside me again. Right now, I didn't trust myself to speak.

I moved on to the next photograph, where the mist now hovered over one of the stones. "It can't be the lens," I said, "If it was, the mark would always be in the same place and it isn't. Look."

Again, he leaned over my shoulder as I flicked from the first picture, to the second, where the white mist had moved to the right-hand side. On the third picture, it again hovered over Greg, but this time it was in the center.

"Okay. It's a bit of fluff. You must have had some fluff on the lens and it got blown around."

"*What?* Oh come on, Greg, that's more ridiculous than admitting there might just be something supernatural going on here."

"Only because you want there to be, Alex. To the rest of us sane human beings, we see a bit of fluff. Give me the camera and I'll prove it to you."

I unplugged it from the computer and handed it to him.

He examined it closely. "I can't see anything, but it probably rubbed off in your pocket on the way back. Come to think of it, that's probably how it got on to the camera in the first place. You really should keep it in the carrying case.

"It's too bulky for my pocket and I wanted both hands free."

"Anyway, that's no doubt what happened."

I turned my back on him and continued to study the photographs, one at a time. As each one flashed up on the screen, I focused on the white mark.

When I reached the final one, the mark had grown bigger, closer and clearer. I stared at the enlarged version, at the unmistakable image looking out at me.

"Greg, you have to see this."

He was flicking through the TV channels. "What now?"

"The image. It's much clearer on the last picture. It's the one you took of me."

He sighed, threw the remote on the bed and came over. He peered at the enlarged segment. I heard him suck in his breath.

"Well? What do you see?"

"I'll admit it does have some features that could be construed as a sort of mouth and two eyes, but they're really just black circles."

"Those black circles are very familiar to me, and now, at last, you've seen them too."

He stared at me, disbelievingly for a second. "You don't seriously mean… Alex, are you sure you didn't hit your head last night?"

"I'm deadly serious."

I turned back to the screen and took a long, hard look at the familiar image. I had no idea what she was doing there, but, for some reason I had captured her on camera for the first time and I was as certain as I could be that it had been her voice that had told me to get out of there.

My specter.

Chapter Six

Jonas Devine frowned as he touched his stepdaughter's shoulder. "Grace, my child, whatever's the matter?"

Grace peered at him through eyes blurred by tears that would not stop flowing. Could she tell him? Wouldn't he think her childish, sobbing so much over a silly toy? Would he understand that it was the destruction of the only thing left of her father that caused her so much anguish?

She took a ragged breath and shook her head. Even if she did tell him, she had no proof that Adrian had smashed Lydia. Just certain knowledge borne of well-founded suspicion.

Jonas puffed on his pipe while he waited for her to reply. In the grate, the winter fire crackled and spat, while a furious rainstorm beat a tattoo on the windows.

"Grace?"

With a great effort, Grace stemmed the flow of tears. She took a clean handkerchief from her pocket, dried her eyes and blew her nose.

Jonas Devine tapped out his pipe on the hearth and uncrossed his legs. Then he leaned back in his chair and steepled his fingers. Grace studied him. He had long elegant fingers, like the hands of a pianist or an artist. Indeed, he was an accomplished musician. She often heard the strains of Mozart or Chopin filter upwards to her room from the drawing room. Not that Grace knew much about music, but her stepfather seemed to be able to squeeze every last drop of emotion from each piece he played.

Jonas coughed. "Grace, I know things can't be easy for you. Losing your father and now your mother… I miss her too." His voice cracked a little. "I want you to know that you will always have a home here and that I regard you as my own daughter. I hope you know that?"

Grace felt a lump wedge firmly in her throat and didn't trust herself to speak. She nodded, and a stray strand of hair detached itself from her ponytail and fell across her face. She tucked it behind her ear.

"I also want you to know that I am aware of Adrian's poor behavior towards you. I shall be speaking to him about it later." Jonas sighed. "I'm afraid he carries too much of his mother in his blood. She could be very…volatile at times. So unlike your dear mother…" He choked and Grace noticed a tear streak down his cheek.

In a wild impulse, she raced over and knelt in front of him. He cradled her head and she clasped his knee.

"My dear girl. How I wish your mother was still here."

"So do I, Stepfather. I miss her so much, it hurts."

Grace stayed with her stepfather for the rest of that evening until her bedtime when she placed a feather-light kiss on his cheek and departed for her own room.

At her door, she removed the key from her pocket and inserted it into the lock. At least this time she shouldn't be in for any more nasty shocks.

She stepped inside and peered around anxiously. Everything was neat and just as she had left it. Lydia, she knew, lay wrapped in tissue paper, tucked safely back in her drawer. If only she'd left her there in the first place. However ruined she might be, Grace still hadn't the heart to toss her out like a piece of worthless rubbish.

A few weeks later, with Christmas and New Year behind them, a week of gale-force winds, heavy snowfall and freezing temperatures had finally given way to a bright and crisp late January morning. Grace breathed in the clear air that chilled so much it burned her lungs, but tasted sweeter than nectar. She stood on the porch and watched her breath form clouds in front of her. Saturday, so no school. Mr. Angus had taken himself off to visit his sister on a remote farm on the other side of the island, despite Jonas's warnings about treacherous roads and icy patches that could fell even the tutor's trusty horse.

Grace had waved him off and he had tipped his hat to her. A little shudder of pleasure had swum up from her stomach. Looked at in a certain angle, when the light was right, Mr. Angus was quite an attractive man.

Her heart lifted by the glorious weather, Grace stared out over the snow-covered grasslands, to the lake that shimmered ghostly in the sunlight, its white blanket in sharp contrast to the vivid blue sky. No sign of the black and dark gray clouds of the past few weeks. Today, she might even wear her brand-new bonnet—chocolate brown and tied up with matching silk ribbons. She had never had a fur hat before and this one felt soft as a kitten. Her first grown-up hat—a special Christmas present from her stepfather.

She had seen the scowl on Adrian's face as his father beamed with pleasure when he handed it over to her. She longed to wear it outside, perhaps to the kirk, but the weather had been so awful, she didn't want to risk ruining it. Today, though…

Robert tugged her sleeve. "Penny for them."

"Hello, Robert, what are you up to this morning?"

The boy, who looked young for his ten years, kicked a piece of mud off the porch step and thrust his hands into the pockets of his coat.

"Nothing much. Adrian wants to go down to the lake and skim stones on the ice."

At the mention of his name, all the lightness of spirit Grace had just been feeling sank into her boots. "Oh," she said and resumed her gaze over the lake, hoping to recapture some of her earlier inner peace. It didn't work.

"Adrian doesn't like to go alone so I expect he'll drag me along with him. I'd rather stay in and read a book. Is that what you'll be doing?" He looked up at her, his eyes like an innocent puppy.

"I may do that, or I may go out for a walk. You could come with me, if you like."

Robert's face lit up and then fell again. "I'll probably get a drubbing from Adrian if I do that."

The two watched a solitary duck fly low over the lake.

"He's looking for an unfrozen bit," Robert said. "Father told me he couldn't remember the lake as solid as this."

Grace only half-heard him. Suddenly, she could keep it in no longer. "Robert, why does Adrian hate me so much? I mean, my mother was your stepmother too, but you and I have always been friends, haven't we?"

Robert fidgeted, as if uncomfortable with her question. "Adrian loved our mother very much. He misses her."

"I miss mine too." Automatically, she touched the locket. It gave her some comfort.

Robert placed his small hand protectively over Grace's. "I know," he said, softly. "I do too. I miss her. She was the only mother I've ever known." His face clouded over and his eyes grew huge. "Oh, promise you won't tell Adrian I said that. He'd kill me!"

Robert bit his lip and seemed to be debating with himself whether or not to tell Grace something. He looked around, perhaps checking that they really were alone.

"Grace, Adrian isn't like other boys. There's... something. I mean...he told me that, on her death bed, our mother passed on something to him."

"What?"

Robert shook his head. "He won't tell me. He said she knew she was dying and had to pass on a secret so it would be safe for the next generation. He said it's a secret power and one day he may have to use it."

"That's all very mysterious."

The boy's face blanched. "Oh, I think it's much more than that. I don't know why, but I think it's something evil. Black magic or something."

Grace laughed. "Oh, don't be so fanciful, Robert. You'll be saying he's a witch next."

"Witches are all female, aren't they?"

Grace frowned. "Well, a wizard then. Like Merlin in the tales of King Arthur." Robert seemed to ponder this for a minute. "Maybe that's it. Perhaps he is a wizard.

But I think the power he's got is only to do harm. I don't think it's good magic."

Grace stared at him. He really seemed to believe this stuff. Whatever nonsense was Adrian filling his head with? Goodness, the boy was trembling now.

A wave of pure anger shot through her. "He's really scared you, hasn't he?" She was about to reassure Robert when she heard footsteps and felt the young boy tense.

From around the corner of the house, Adrian sauntered towards them. Grace briefly wondered where he had been so early in the morning, but had no inclination to question him. She preferred to say as little as possible in his presence. Especially since Mr. Angus had warned her about him.

He ignored her and spoke to his brother. "I see Bull's gone off to see his lady friend. He's been champing at the bit all these weeks, so the minute the sky clears, off he goes."

"He's gone to visit his sister in St. Magnus," Robert said.

Adrian laughed, but it sounded false. Mirthless. Grace stared straight ahead, not wanting to meet his eyes.

"You idiot! He's got a girlfriend. He's had her for years. Every chance he gets, he's over there, and, I bet they're not discussing the weather either!"

"What do you mean?" Robert asked.

"Never mind. You're too young. Won't be long before Grace finds out though."

She flinched. Although she had no clue what Adrian was hinting at, she knew from his tone that it must be something sinful, something his father wouldn't approve of.

"Come on, baby brother, let's go down to the lake and throw stones. Let's see who can skim theirs the farthest across the ice. Grace, you can come too if you like."

Grace jerked her head around. He must be mocking her. Adrian had never invited her to do anything before. But his smile seemed genuine enough.

"I..." She didn't know what to do. Had his father spoken to him? Was he holding out the proverbial olive branch?

"I've been rather horrible to you recently. I'd like to make amends. Will you come with us?"

Grace couldn't find any words and, even if she could, she doubted her voice would have worked.

Adrian continued to smile at her. He seemed to genuinely want to be friendly all of a sudden. Why? She wracked her brain but could come up with no reason. There might be nothing in this simple gesture for him. Then Mr. Angus's warning came into her mind. But she wouldn't be alone with him. Granted there wouldn't be another adult, but Robert would be there. Surely, he wouldn't do anything untoward in front of his younger brother.

"Come on, Grace," Adrian said, with no hint of impatience. "What do you say? You could wear your new hat."

That clinched it. "Yes, I'd be delighted. I'll just be five minutes."

She picked up her skirts, dashed inside and scampered up the stairs to her bedroom.

The promised five minutes later, she rejoined the boys on the porch, warmly wrapped in her scarlet winter coat over her white, floral-patterned dress. Her feet were shod in her shiny, black button boots and her hands were snug in her woolen mittens. On her head, she had proudly tied her new hat.

Robert stared in surprise and Adrian appraised her. "My, my, what a transformation. Quite the grown-up in that hat, aren't you?"

Grace squashed all the warning voices in her head and smiled. She felt warm and content. Could this be the start of a new relationship between them? She prayed so. She had only ever wanted a brother she could look up to and Adrian could so easily have been that brother, if he had ever let her anywhere near. Today though, he seemed to have changed. She decided that his father must have reasoned with him and, somehow, managed to get him to see sense.

Adrian beckoned to her. "Come on then, let's go."

Grace lowered herself down the steps off the porch, taking care not to slip on the flagstones. On the grass, it proved easier to walk, as long as she watched where she was going. The icy grass crunched as the three made their way towards the lake.

Robert chatted about Mr. Angus. "I can't imagine Bull with a girlfriend. I mean, what do they do? Play games?"

Adrian burst out laughing. "Oh, Robert, wait till you're a little older and you won't have to ask such questions, will he, Grace?"

Grace's cheeks burned and not just from the cold air. "I...really don't know."

This just made Adrian laugh harder as they arrived at the water's edge. The lake shimmered and no waves rippled at the edges.

"Gosh." Robert picked up a stone. "It looks like a mirror."

"Yes," Grace said. "And farther in, it looks like it's covered in frosted icing."

"Will the fishes freeze?" Robert sounded anxious.

"No," Adrian said. "They just swim deeper. The lake's not frozen all the way through. Just at the top."

"Could we skate on it?" he asked.

"Probably. If we had any skates, which we don't. I'll have to speak to Father about it. What do you think, Grace? Would you like to skate?"

Grace could think of nothing worse. She shook her head. "No, indeed. The ice might crack and I'd fall in. I can't swim."

"The ice is much too thick for that. Look."

Adrian picked up a flat stone and threw it underarm. It skimmed and skidded across the ice, out of sight. There was no resounding 'plop'.

"See? Solid ice. That stone's lying out there on top of the lake. Your turn now, Robert."

His brother took aim and copied his brother. His stone also skidded across the frozen lake, making a whooshing sound until they could neither hear nor see it. Once again, no 'plop'.

"Now it's your turn, Grace," Adrian said as he bent down and picked up a light weight, flat stone. He handed it to her and she held it in her right hand, glad of the wool separating her skin from its freezing surface.

She eyed up the lake and took aim. Her clumsy throw sent the stone spinning into the air, before it crashed down onto the lake surface with a loud 'crack'.

"Goodness, Grace, we'll never make a bowler of you, will we?" Adrian and Robert laughed. Seeing their smiling faces, Grace started to laugh too. Then stopped, as in one swift move, Adrian grabbed her hat and ripped it from her head. He flung it out onto the lake and Grace watched in horror as it skidded along the surface.

Robert's laughter turned to shock. "Adrian, what did you do that for?"

His brother shrugged. "It was only a bit of fun. She can go and get it now."

"No, she can't. It might not be safe. She might fall in."

"Well, if she won't go and get it, she'll have to explain to Father where his precious gift went."

"But *you* threw it onto the lake, Adrian. You should be the one to go and fetch it. You heard Grace. She's frightened of the ice. She can't swim."

"She doesn't have to swim. She just has to walk. Don't you, Grace?"

All his earlier friendliness had vanished. Now Grace knew he had planned this all along. This was the reason he had been nice to her—and why he had asked her along. Her heart beat loudly and her breath came in short gasps as she realized she would have to go out onto that ice if she was ever to see her hat again.

But the stones hadn't sunk. She knew she weighed far heavier than a stone, however slim she might be, but the ice really did look thick. As she peered down into the shallows, it seemed to be one solid block. But how deep would it be once she had left the safety of the shore?

"Come along, Grace, go and get it. We need to get back for lunch. Father will be waiting."

Grace took a deep breath and tested the ice with her right foot. It didn't crack. She lifted her left foot, but try as she might, she couldn't will it to leave the bank.

Adrian tutted. "Dear me, what a cowardly little girl you are. Scared of a bit of ice. It's only a few feet out. Get a move on or I'll push you."

Robert stared, white-faced, and Grace marked the contrast between his innocent expression and the grim darkness of his elder brother. At that moment, Adrian's face seemed to twist out of proportion and another, more frightening expression took over. In that second, Grace didn't know who she feared most—the ice or Adrian.

She loved that hat so much and Stepfather would be hurt if he knew she had been so careless as to lose it. One way or another, she had to go out on that ice and pray the sun hadn't begun its work of melting it.

One mammoth effort of willpower dragged her left foot to stand next to its partner on the ice.

Robert whimpered on the bank. "Oh, be careful, Grace."

She tried to smile at him to reassure him but her lips wouldn't work. Grace took another wobbly step and then another. She looked back. Shimmering ice lay between her and the bank and all around her. In the distance, patches of it gleamed like crystal. They seemed a different texture somehow. The hat lay on one of those.

She took another step and, in the distance, heard a faint cracking sound. It didn't seem close. She must keep going. Now, roughly halfway between the shore and the hat, she couldn't turn back. She had to keep on and the sooner she retrieved her prize, the sooner she could get her feet back on safe ground.

She turned her back on the bank and ignored Robert's voice calling out to her. As she neared the hat, anger welled up inside her. Anger against Adrian. He had gone too far this time. Much too far. When she got home, she would tell his father precisely what he had done. How he had duped her and put her life in danger. Stepfather would be angry. Very angry. Maybe angry enough to send Adrian away at last. Mr. Angus said he should be in a proper boarding school. Maybe they'd be able to teach him discipline and self-control. She didn't really care as long as she didn't have to live with him anymore.

The hat lay just a few feet away. Maybe she could reach it if she bent down and stretched as far as she could. The fewer steps she took, the better.

She wobbled as she crouched and stretched out her hand. A ribbon hovered, tantalizingly close. She touched it with the tip of her middle finger but couldn't stretch enough to grab it. One more small step should do it. She took it and heard another crack. Closer this time. Much closer.

She could see the hat and the reason the ice looked different here. Some of it had melted in the sunlight and the hat was lying in half an inch of water. Ruined. Hot tears stung her cheeks as she reached for it. Her fingers found the sodden ribbons and she scooped it up. Another loud crack. Another. And another and...

She heard Robert's frantic cry. "Look out!"

The ice lurched under Grace's feet. She watched the crack in horrified fascination as it sped, snake-like, towards her. She could do nothing to prevent what must surely follow.

A judder.

A sickening crunch.

She took a massive breath and was plunged through the shattered ice. The freezing water forced the air out of her lungs as she sank under, only to resurface. She choked, shivered. Screamed for help. She kicked her rapidly numbing legs, flailed with her arms. Anything to keep afloat. She must get out of this water. Now. Before she went under for the last time.

Around her, the ice broke up into small floes and she tried to grab hold of one, but they were too unstable. None was big enough to take her weight, made worse by her drenched coat that dragged her down.

In desperation, she clutched and clawed at the ice around her.

On the bank, Robert was running frantically backwards and forwards. He remonstrated with his brother. She could see his small arms waving up and down, pointing at her. Pointing at Adrian. But the older boy just stood and watched. She could sense his triumphant look.

The weight of her coat dragged her down again. If only she could get it off, but her fingers fumbled as she discarded her mittens. Only seconds had passed, but it seemed like hours. Finally, she managed to undo the buttons and drag the coat off her, with strength she didn't even know she possessed. But now, she could no longer feel her hands and legs. Her consciousness drifted and nothing seemed real anymore.

She struggled to inhale into lungs that were seizing up. Her vision blurred and a loud hissing rang in her ears.

Then, she felt something soft touch her cheek. The hat.

Grace opened her mouth and tried to speak, but no words would come out. Her blood was turning to ice and when she saw her hands, they were blue. They seemed to belong to someone else. She no longer had a body, just a terrified mind in a frozen shell.

As she started to sink for the third time, the water lapped at her chin, but she no longer felt cold. Just angry and resentful, vengeful for the loss of a life she would now never know. She managed to tighten her numb hand around the locket and shut her eyes for the last time.

The water closed over her head and her last thought drifted back across the lake, to the one person she meant it for.

I curse you, Adrian Devine. I curse you for all time. May you never know peace or happiness all the days of your life…

Chapter Seven

The rain returned the following morning and Greg seemed relieved to have the perfect excuse to get back to work. Or maybe my paranoia had kicked in again.

Although we had both apologized for the previous evening, a lingering resentment hovered in the air. I knew what I could see on the photographs. Greg was equally convinced I had it wrong. We were in a never ending circle, so no point in discussing it further.

But why had my specter followed me here? Why had she manifested on the photographs, where she could be seen hovering, not just over me, but Greg as well? And if that *had* been her voice, why would she order me to get out of there? Or maybe her warning was directed at my need to help Grace? Questions, endless questions—and not one answer in sight.

After breakfast, Greg went straight back to our room, grabbed his laptop and disappeared off to the residents' lounge. He hadn't even bothered to ask what plans I had for the day. He probably assumed I'd go off to the museum, but today I had other ideas, plans that sent butterflies fluttering backwards and forwards across my stomach. Today I had decided I would try and find out the secrets of the painting.

The wardrobe was a simple, white, chipboard affair. Nothing sinister about it. Not unless you knew what lurked on its top shelf. I stood a few feet away, staring at it, my palms sweaty and heart pounding.

Oh come on, this is ridiculous. It can't harm you.

But somehow I knew it could. Maybe that's why my specter was here, to warn me to leave it alone. Or maybe she wanted to encourage me to use it. Was she here now? I scanned the room, but nothing lurked in any corner. The camera lay on its side on the dressing table. Never had a lens been cleaned so thoroughly. Despite my fear, a smile crept to my lips. If anything appeared on any photos now, Greg would have to believe me, wouldn't he?

I inched my way closer to the wardrobe until the handle was within my grasp. Strange that I had opened it without thinking a couple of hours earlier, retrieved my jeans and a T-shirt, closed it... But then I wasn't reaching for the painting as I now did. I stretched up on tiptoe and rummaged under the spare blanket until my hands closed on the rolled up canvas. At that moment, my fingers tingled, like pins and needles.

Stop it!

I tugged at the painting and it emerged from its hiding place. I slid the rubber band off and hesitated; both my hands now tingled and the canvas felt damp.

It's just your stupid imagination.

But it felt awfully real to me.

I grabbed the camera, a book, the hair dryer and one of my shoes, so I would have something to hold down each corner of the canvas. Then, I knelt down, took a deep breath and started to unroll it, pinning the top and bottom left corners with the shoe and the hair dryer. Slowly, the painting was revealed and I anchored down all four corners on the floor.

The artist had captured all the texture and colors of the lake. The oil paint gleamed and I couldn't resist touching it, surprised to find my finger felt cold and wet, yet when I looked at it, there was no sign of moisture.

Grace floated there, suspended, her eyes closed.

I stared at it while seconds became minutes and my fears drained away. This was just a painting. It didn't hold any secrets, except the mystery of who had painted it, why, and what it had been doing stuffed in a drawer. The chance of me finding out the answers to any of my questions was remote at best. Even if I did, would it further my quest to save Grace and help her pass over? Unlikely.

I made my decision. I would return the painting to the museum now. Of course, I would have to do it surreptitiously and that would mean returning upstairs to the dreaded gallery. Unless, of course, I just hid it somewhere else, downstairs, while Duncan was occupied elsewhere. Great idea!

Not so great idea.

I remembered he had told me he had switched off the CCTV cameras upstairs—but downstairs? He would see my every move. No. I couldn't avoid it. I would have to take it back up to the gallery. Best do it now, while I had the confidence of seeing the painting do absolutely nothing. I sighed and slid the camera off the corner of the picture.

It flew out of my hand and spun around by itself, on the carpet.

"Oh my God!" Adrenalin pumped through my veins.

I watched, terrified, as the camera set off a series of rapid flashes and clicked frame after frame. I jumped up, just as it stopped and toppled over, as if someone had casually tossed it aside.

I stared at the silent camera until a noise distracted me. The picture, which had remained a little curled, despite its restraints, was flattening itself out. Gradually, the hair dryer, book and shoe slid off, as the canvas appeared to develop more strength and its texture morphed.

Then I heard it. Like someone flailing around in a pool. My eyes misted over and I blinked. Suddenly, freezing water swept my breath away. It numbed my legs and I kicked out, unable to remember how to swim. I sank underwater. All around me, murky shades of green, blue and muddy brown. I opened my mouth to scream and water rushed in. Disgusting, tainted water, tasting of weeds and slime. My arms flailed and somehow broke the surface. I gasped for air, only for my nose to fill with the sickly sweet, cloying stench of putrefaction. I heard cries coming from far away, warning calls of seabirds, mixed with a child's screams.

I felt a nudge at my shoulder and screamed as a skeletal arm floated next to me, its ghost-white fingers pointing upwards. I screamed again and, in front of me, as if through glass, I saw the empty hotel room. I struggled to move, but now I pushed against an invisible wall that separated me from my own world. At least I wasn't sinking anymore. I hung suspended, just like Grace in that painting. Then I knew. Grace wanted me to feel what she had felt. The same paralyzing fear. She had succeeded. Any second now and I would sink back down into the depths of this stinking lake of death. No one would know. No one would ever find me.

A mist enveloped me and the next thing I knew, I was lying on carpet, my throat raw from coughing up the foul water. Choking and shivering with cold and fear, I managed to sit up. Still the rotten stench filled my nose and, when I looked down at myself, stinking weeds were tangled around my legs.

The painting lay in front of me, curled into a loose cylinder. Gingerly, I unrolled it again. This time, nothing. No tingling or moisture. Grace still floated there, her eyes closed.

As if in a dream, I reached over for the rubber band, then rolled the painting tighter and secured it. I would need to shower and change before I left, and probably bin the clothes I was wearing, but I'd hang on to them until Greg came up. I was intrigued how he would explain them away.

But by the time I reached the bathroom, I was perfectly dry. The weeds had vanished and I smelled pleasantly of body spray, just as if all of that had been meant for me alone and no one else was to know.

Back in the bedroom, the painting still lay where I had left it, on the dressing table. On the floor, the shoe, hair dryer, book and camera lay scattered.

Despite my jitters, I had to take action straightaway and download the pictures, but Greg had the laptop. Well, okay then, let him upload the photographs and we would see them for the first time, together.

Without another thought, I pushed the painting back into its hiding place. I really didn't want to be anywhere near it, but, at the same time, it had become clear that its presence mattered in achieving my goal, although I hoped and prayed it wouldn't put me through another ordeal like that again.

I grabbed the USB cable, handbag and camera, and shut the bedroom door firmly behind me.

Greg looked up as I strode up to him in the lounge. We were alone.

"You look flushed," he said.

"I feel it," I replied.

"What's happened?"

At least he sounded as if he cared, and my annoyance melted away. He and I had no business falling out. We loved each other too much.

I thrust the camera and USB cable at him. "I know you're busy, but would you upload these pictures for me?"

"What have you been photographing? I thought you were upstairs." He plugged the USB into his laptop and it started loading up.

"I was. But something...well, you'll see for yourself."

Although just *what* he would see, I hadn't a clue.

Images not much bigger than thumbnails amassed on the screen and, when they had finished, Greg saved them. A couple of clicks later, he had created a slideshow of the pictures taken that morning. Ten of them, all identical.

"What the hell's that?" Greg stared at the screen as pictures of dark blue-green water skipped by, one after the other.

I watched, incredulously, over his shoulder. Only dim light penetrated the murky water. How on earth had the camera captured that? But then, how on earth had the pictures been snapped in the first place? The colors reminded me of the painting, and of my ordeal, as I struggled to survive in the freezing waters of the lake.

"Where were you when you took these?"

My voice was no more than a whisper. "I didn't take them."

"What do you mean, you didn't take them? I didn't."

"I mean, I was looking at the painting and the camera was on the floor. Then it started snapping and..."

Greg had turned from the screen, with a horrified look on his face. "Do you realize that none of what you've just said makes any sense?"

I nodded.

"Alex, I'm really getting worried about you. Ever since we've been here and you've been investigating this Devine family, you seem to be losing touch with reality."

And I thought I'd managed to keep a tight lid on it.

Greg stared hard at me and I felt increasingly uncomfortable. "Maybe we should go back home," he said.

My heart leaped at the prospect and then sank again. How could I leave? I was no closer to saving Grace than when I had arrived. And, after today, I was even more determined to end her suffering.

"I'm fine, Greg, honestly."

"Then what is all this about?" He made a sweeping gesture towards the laptop, which had now stopped on the last frame. "And what's this about a painting?"

That had been a mistake. How could I explain it?

I waved his concerns away with a sweep of my hand. "Just ignore me. I tried to take snaps of a painting Duncan lent me from the museum. They didn't come out right."

He wouldn't be fobbed off that easily. "But you said the camera took the pictures. Not you."

"I was joking. I didn't want you to think I was such a lousy photographer."

I concentrated on keeping my features steady and retaining eye contact. It seemed the longest time until he broke off and looked back at the screen. He shut down the program and ejected the USB.

"I know there's something you're not telling me, Alex, and I don't know whether I should be angry or just plain worried."

I retrieved the camera and its lead. "I've told you. I'm fine. Nothing to worry about. Now, I'll have to get back to the museum. Duncan will wonder where I've got to."

"Best take his painting back too."

I nodded and left him to his work.

Duncan was showing some people around when I arrived. He smiled and waved at me and I wished I had brought the wretched picture with me. I could have taken it back upstairs, thrust it in its drawer and been back down before anything untoward could happen. The sound of other human voices would have served to give me the courage I needed. Too late now.

I needed to speak to Duncan, so I meandered around the glass cabinets, staring at, but not seeing, the exhibits. A few minutes later, he came to join me. "And how are you today?"

"Confused and a bit worried, if I'm honest," I said. "Some very strange things have been happening to me and I don't know what to do about them."

"Want to tell me?"

I nodded. "I think, right now, you're the only person who'll understand or believe me. I need to know I'm not going out of my mind."

We sat in our usual spot and Duncan listened to my story. I held nothing back. If he thought I'd gone mad, then so be it. But, from his expression and the way he nodded, he was taking me seriously. Either that or he would be up for an Oscar next year.

Finally, I brought him up to date with the strange photographs. The couple who had been there when I arrived wandered past us, probably on their way upstairs. They smiled and I smiled back.

Good luck, I thought.

"You seem to have a strong connection to Grace," Duncan said. "But you're not related to her in any way."

"No. But I'm sure it's all linked up with my specter. I don't know how, but maybe it's just because I do have some psychic ability. I must have, or I wouldn't see my ghost. I just can't understand why she's here and why she allowed herself to be photographed. And did she warn me to leave? If so, did she mean the burial chamber, or the island? And why did she apparently attach herself to Greg as well as me when, up till now, she's always kept herself away from him?"

"He's in denial, you say? Greg, I mean."

"Oh, yes. Won't believe a word of it. He's convinced the anomaly on the photographs is a bit of fluff and that I took some terrible pictures of…" I stopped myself. I hadn't admitted to Duncan just which picture I'd been handling. I had merely said the camera had gone off by itself ten times, photographing the carpet. "He has a complete block when it comes to belief in anything he can't see, touch, hear and smell."

"Aye, it's common enough." Duncan went over to a chest of drawers a few feet away. "I've been wondering whether or not to show this to you. When we talked the other day, it brought back memories of conversations I had with my grandfather years ago, when I was in my teens. I suddenly remembered an old diary he gave me. Have a look."

From a drawer, he pulled out a small pocket diary, complete with an attached pencil, much used and sharpened until it had reduced to roughly half its original size.

"Have a look at the date."

Embossed in gold on the leather cover was '1902'.

"Open it, have a look at January 24th and then read on from there."

"This was your grandfather's diary?" The childish scrawl was a little difficult to decipher.

"Yes, I'm afraid handwriting was never one of his greatest strengths. But then, which doctor's is?"

I smiled and flicked through the pages, until I arrived at January 24th.

Terrible day. Poor Grace drowned and it's all Adrian's fault. Told Father and he was furious. Now Adrian will be banished. And a good job too!

January 25th was blank, but then on January 26th, Robert had written, *Father has decided. Adrian is to leave the island with his fare, one way, and two hundred pounds in his pocket. Father told him he would have to make it last because he would never see another penny. Adrian is very angry and I keep out of his way. He has that look in his eye again. The one he had when Grace drowned.*

More blank pages followed, until I reached an entry for February 8th. *Adrian left today. Good riddance. He has been fearfully horrid to the cook and she fell down the back stairs and broke her ankle. He laughed. Did any boy ever have such an evil brother? But not anymore. He's gone. Hoorah!*

I closed the diary. "Am I reading this correctly? Did Robert think Adrian was responsible for the cook's accident?"

"Oh, yes, I'm sure of it. Grandfather believed Adrian had inherited some psychic or demonic powers from his mother. He told me so himself. And he wasn't afraid to use them either."

"Robert certainly hated his brother."

"Till the day he died."

"Do you remember anything else?"

"Just one thing. And it's in the diary. A passing mention and that's it. Have a look at October 20th. I don't think I'd ever read it until yesterday."

I flicked through and found the page.

The minister called to see Father today. He told him he had been in Edinburgh for some conference of churches. Rev. McCloud said he'd seen Adrian, very down at heel. Father raised his voice and asked the minister never to mention that name again. Then he shut the door and I heard no more.

"And that's all there is?"

Duncan nodded. "As far as I know my grandfather never kept another diary. I don't really know why he kept this one, except, maybe because it contained his last memories of Grace."

"He must have loved her very much."

"Undoubtedly he did. And he never forgave his brother for taking her away from him. In Robert's eyes, Adrian was a cold-blooded murderer and should have been hanged for it."

"He's given us a clue though. If I'm to find Adrian's closest descendant, at least I know where I need to start looking. Of course, my research may lead me back to you. You are his great-nephew after all."

"True. Well, for what it's worth—and just in case—on behalf of my great-uncle Adrian, I forgive you, Grace, for the curse you placed on him."

We didn't move for a few seconds. Nothing happened. In my heart I never expected it to. There had to be someone closer related to Adrian, and I had to find him or her.

Duncan sighed. He knew too. "It was worth a try. Use my laptop if you like."

Five minutes later, I had already discovered that there were over two hundred people with the surname 'Devine' on the electoral roll in the Edinburgh area. If I wanted to trace their contact details, I would have to buy a subscription to the website and, with so many, it wouldn't be cheap. I felt my spirits sink.

"You could try the old-fashioned method," Duncan said. "Go through the phone directory, and hope the right one isn't ex-directory."

"Do you have an Edinburgh phone book?"

"No. But I rather think the library does."

"Thanks, Duncan. I'll try them."

At least it would weed out some of the chaff. Along the way, I stopped in the newsagent's and bought a shorthand notebook. With all those candidates to choose from, I needed to make sure I didn't go over the same ground twice. I would need to be organized.

The library had the same timeless quality as the museum. Here, peace reigned and I had the impression the librarian wouldn't have tolerated the level of noise I was used to from my own library.

Seated in a comfortable chair, with the directory in front of me, I opened my notebook and faithfully copied down all the Devines, along with their addresses and phone numbers. Photocopying had proved useless, as the resulting copy was virtually illegible.

Back at the hotel, Greg was in a sunny mood.

"How did your day go?" he asked as we sat at dinner.

"Good. I found out the Devine family may have descendants in Edinburgh."

"Oh?"

"It seems that's where the black sheep son, Adrian, ended up."

"You're really into this, aren't you? I meant what I said earlier though. I really am concerned you're getting a bit carried away with it."

"I know and I'm really sorry about earlier. I didn't explain myself properly that's all. I'm thoroughly enjoying this research. It's giving me something interesting to focus on and, with the redundancy and all the stress these past months, it's a welcome relief I can tell you." I sounded convincing; I'd give myself a round of applause for that. I even managed to half-convince myself that this really was just a bit of harmless fun, so it would be hardly surprising if Greg bought my version of events. A sudden thought flashed into my mind. "How would you feel about going there? To Edinburgh, I mean?"

His eyes widened. "You mean cut short our holiday here?"

I nodded. "Or maybe take a few days out, go to Edinburgh and then come back again."

Greg shook his head. "I don't think Laurence would be too happy about that. It would mess him around too much."

"Okay then, let's cut it short here and finish the rest of our holiday in Edinburgh."

"When do you want to go?"

"Tomorrow."

Before we left, I had two remaining tasks. First, I needed to say goodbye to Duncan. He seemed taken aback when I told him what we had decided.

"I thought your husband was skeptical about these things," he said.

"He is, but I haven't told him about that side of it. I just told him I was fascinated by the Devine family history and wanted to find out more about what happened to Adrian." Even as I spoke, I felt guilty. I sounded devious because I was devious.

"I hope you're doing the right thing," Duncan said. "I've always been glad to know that, wherever he finally ended up, at least Adrian Devine and any children he might have had are a good few hundred miles away."

I was sure Duncan shivered then. "Just be careful, Alex. I've always been brought up to believe that there was something strange about Adrian. Something he may have inherited from his mother, but definitely something I would call evil."

Evil. That word seemed to fit around Adrian Devine's shoulders as snugly as a scarf. I shuddered.

With promises to keep in touch, I left the museum and went on to my final task. A visit to the Devine family vault in the kirk of St Andrew.

I trudged up the steep slope of the High Street and turned down a small, narrow street, with high-walled buildings framing either side. My trainers made no sound on the flagstones and recent rain glistened and formed shallow pools where the stones were worn.

Fortunately the church was unlocked and I assumed it probably remained that way for most of the day and night. They didn't need to fear thieves here as much as on the mainland. I unlatched the wooden door that issued an echoing creak as I passed through it. Inside, the welcoming aromas of beeswax and spring flowers from an ornate arrangement reminded me of Sundays in church in my childhood. Warm though the smells were, this church had the same lack of heating I remembered from those days. I pulled my jacket tighter around me.

Wrought iron gates marked the entry to the Devine vault. I opened them. Inside, a large marble wall plaque listed the members of the Devine family who had been laid to rest here. Jonas, his two wives, son Robert and stepdaughter Grace. Adrian was conspicuous by his absence.

There was no mention of him on his father's tomb either. The pink marble sarcophagus described Jonas as 'beloved father of Robert and late stepdaughter Grace.'

Margarita's tomb listed her as, 'wife of Jonas and mother of Robert'. While Agnes was portrayed as 'devoted wife of Jonas and loving mother of Grace and stepson Robert.'

So Jonas had never wavered. He had written Adrian out of his family's history as if he had never existed.

I found Grace's memorial, right next to her mother. Smaller than her mother's sarcophagus, hers was in white marble. *Grace Elizabeth, beloved daughter of the late Agnes and much loved stepdaughter of Jonas. Tragically drowned January 24th, 1902, aged 14. Grant her peace.*

I lingered there for maybe ten minutes and tried to connect with any form of residual energy, but found none. Not a spark of life lingered in that hall of death. By now, I was as sure as I could be that no restless spirit roamed around here. Wherever Grace was, I wouldn't find her in this place.

But then, she wasn't at rest, was she? Not yet. Not ever if I didn't fulfill my promise to her. Inside me, something moved. Something intangible, but which made my stomach heave.

Chapter Eight

With all flights full, our ferry and rail journey was tortuous. Seven and a half hours on a train gives you ample time to think. We changed at Inverness and that was probably the only time Greg and I spoke. Not because we had argued, but he had his head in a book and I was too preoccupied.

I also wondered if I had brought any of my spirits with me. Was Grace there, in the painting? I had agonized over whether to return it to Duncan in some surreptitious way, but then, as it seemed so closely tied to Grace and my mission, shouldn't I hang on to it a little longer? I could return it when I went back to the island. If I went back.

Greg didn't see me sneak the rolled up canvas into the suitcase. I hid it among my clothes and made sure I packed all my stuff at the bottom of the case. He would have no reason to go rummaging around.

When we arrived at Edinburgh, we decided to walk up to the guest house, just off Charlotte Square in the New Town. I loved Edinburgh's contrasts, its rich history and its mysterious underground vaults. I had promised Greg that we would do some sightseeing and he had promised not to work all the time.

We found a little Italian restaurant for dinner and tucked into delicious pasta, accompanied by a full-bodied, smooth Chianti Classico.

"I never asked you how Laurence took the news," I said as Greg topped up my glass.

He grimaced. "On the surface, very well, but I swear I heard his teeth grinding. The way he wished us a safe journey wasn't terribly convincing."

"Do you think we'd be welcome there again?"

Greg shook his head. "Probably not. Anyway, would you want to go again? I had the impression you couldn't wait to leave there."

"Oh, I don't know. One day…"

"Did you say goodbye to Duncan?"

I nodded and took a mouthful of spicy pasta.

"Changing the subject, how about the tour of the underground city tomorrow?"

I hesitated. I really wanted to make a start on phoning round the Devines, but the tour didn't start until two o'clock, so that still gave me the morning. "That would be great."

"You can have a wander down Princes Street in the morning, while I get a bit of work done. Then we'll meet up for an early lunch and be up at the Royal Mile in good time for the tour. I'll get the tickets sorted online and I bet if I ask them nicely at the guest house, they'll print them off for me."

By the time I'd made my twentieth call, I felt like a parrot. But I plowed on, ticking off names, getting nowhere fast. Nobody I spoke to knew of any relation of theirs called Adrian and I didn't dare dwell on the thought that his nearest descendant might be the offspring of a daughter who had married and changed her name.

At eleven forty-five, I gave up, just after I'd left a message on someone's voicemail.

I hadn't wanted to run the gamut of criticism, skepticism and annoyance that would have been necessary if I had told Greg what I was up to. Let him think I had simply wanted to exchange remote islands in the rain for culture-rich Edinburgh. So much easier than trying to explain my fascination for a ghost he didn't believe in and my determination to help her.

My phone calls had been conducted in a small café, close to the Golden Mile, tucked down a little side street Greg wouldn't have any reason to discover. I finished my third cup of coffee, shoved my phone back in my bag and made my way to the bistro where we had agreed to meet.

Greg was already there, reading a newspaper. He looked up and smiled when he saw me.

"Where are the shopping bags?"

"Didn't see anything I fancied." How easily the lies just tripped off my tongue!

"I got the tickets." He patted his jacket pocket. "We need to be outside the kirk at ten to two."

"Great."

At two o'clock, twenty of us stood in a stiff breeze and listened to the tour guide explain the history of the Closes in the Old Town of Edinburgh and how this labyrinth of shops, homes and all manner of businesses had thrived in the seventeenth century, when they had been open to the air. Then, in the eighteenth century, they began to be submerged underground, as building work continued above them. But deep in their bowels, people continued to live out their lives until the early twentieth century.

Our guide was a lively, enthusiastic girl in her twenties, determined to inject humor and atmosphere into our experience. "Where we are going," she said, "we may hear the cries of walled-up plague victims, or hapless ghosts seeking eternal rest. Mobile phones didn't exist in their time, and we don't want to frighten them. Please check yours is off, or on silent." She beamed at us and there were a few giggles as we dutifully checked our phones.

She then launched into her introduction. According to her, all manner of unspeakable evil had manifested itself in the dark and stinking alleyways. The infamous body snatchers, Burke and Hare, had used the vaults to store corpses. Ghosts and demons were reputed to plague unwary visitors and, as she led us down, off the bustling street, our guide's voice pitched lower as she warned us to stay together, lest stragglers be picked off one by one.

Nervous laughter echoed against the stone walls as we descended below present-day ground level.

A woman in front, dressed in an impractical, long, gypsy style skirt turned to me as we reached the bottom of the stairs. "She's really good, isn't she?" She grinned.

"She's certainly enthusiastic," I replied. "Great sense of atmosphere."

Greg joined me and we dutifully followed our guide, in an orderly crocodile. The narrow Close was lit by wall lamps that cast a dim golden glow over solid stone walls. The uneven street sloped downwards—part cobblestone, part flagstones, with a gutter running along one side.

"Bet that stank in summertime," Greg said.

For a moment, I could almost smell it. I wrinkled my nose. Overhead, washing had been strung across the street. Victorian shirts and combinations, secured by old-fashioned dolly pegs, eerily still, but looking ready for some unseen hand to reach out of a top window and reel them in.

The woman in front of me spoke again. "I can't imagine they would have smelled very fresh, or dried very quickly." I decided she was probably right and imagined miserable years spent scurrying along the stinking streets of this subterranean world. A short life, and a brutal one.

We were led through archways, storerooms and dwellings. Every location had its own folk tale, acted out by the cast, dressed in authentic costumes and armed with boundless enthusiasm.

An entire family would have lived in our last stop: a single room, where the atmosphere hung heavier than elsewhere. A sudden wave of nausea hit me and I retched.

Greg touched my hand. "Are you all right. Alex?"

I swallowed down bile and looked for somewhere I could sit, but this part of the tour involved being plunged into total darkness, while a recorded voice told us of a ghostly sighting. Greg squeezed my hand and I leaned against him.

A fiendish laugh rang around the walls of the room. Light projected a flickering shadow on the wall and the group giggled, gasped and sniggered at all the right moments.

My nausea intensified and I concentrated hard on what I was seeing and hearing, while I swallowed hard in a desperate effort not to vomit.

We were now bathed in a dim, amber light and the woman in front of me turned around, probably to share some further observation with me. But she didn't get that far. Her perpetual grin transformed into a horrified grimace. She screamed. Someone flicked a switch and the room was bathed in light.

"Oh my God. Look at her!" The woman keeled over and her male companion, caught her just in time to break her fall. Four people rushed to assist her.

Greg held me close as the guide dashed over.

She stared at me as if I'd done something to the woman. "Whatever's happened?"

I shook my head.

"She seemed to have some kind of seizure or hallucination," Greg said.

The woman moaned and the guide tried to soothe her. "It's all right. You just fainted."

The woman moaned again and looked vacantly around her. The rest of the group, who were not assisting her, had formed little cliques and chattered amongst themselves, casting glances our way from time to time.

The woman swayed slightly and was supported by her male companion and the guide. Then she caught sight of me and I thought she was going to faint again.

"I remember now." She pointed at me with a trembling finger. "There, above your head. I saw something."

The guide smiled. "You know, a lot of people report seeing visions down here."

The woman ignored her and carried on talking to me. "I don't know what it was. It sort of floated there, right above you. Gray and misty, with two black holes where there should have been eyes."

My specter. Somehow, it had to be. "And a round hole for a mouth?" I said.

She stared at me. "How did you know that?"

"Because I've seen it too," I said.

The guide looked round the assembled group who had now stopped chattering in favor of a far more fascinating scene playing out in front of them.

"Did anyone else see anything above this lady's head?" the guide asked.

There was a general chorus of shaking heads.

Greg whispered in my ear. "Don't say any more about it, Alex. Just leave it for now, please."

My nausea was wearing off now and I could breathe normally. "I need to talk to that woman, Greg. She's the only other person I know who can see her."

"Judging by the look on her face and the fact she's moved herself as far from you as possible, I don't think that's going to be an option."

The woman cast quick glances my way, but I gained the distinct impression she was merely checking I wasn't closing in on her as we all made our way out of the room and into the final section of the Close. At the end, we mounted two flights of steps and I kept my eye firmly on her retreating back. I couldn't let her get away. I had to talk to that woman.

The tour ended in the gift shop and I kept my eye on the blonde head of my target. She seemed to have calmed down now and was laughing and chatting with her male friend. She also seemed to have lost her fear of me, because she didn't cast me a second glance once we emerged above ground. Greg soon became immersed in a book about Burke and Hare, so I sidled up beside her. I would never get a second chance, so I plunged right in.

"I'm sorry to bother you, but have you ever seen anything…out of the ordinary…before?"

She gave a little start and the smile died on her lips. She seemed uncertain whether to speak to me, but, in the end, she nodded. "Once or twice. I went on the other underground tour a couple of days ago. There's a little room there, full of stuffed toys and dolls. They say a little girl called Annie haunts that area. She probably died of plague and, somehow or another, she lost her doll, so she still walks there, looking for it. While we were there, I saw her. Clear as anything."

"And the image you saw floating above me, was that clear?"

She shook her head. "No. It was more misty and undefined. Is amorphous a word?"

I nodded.

"Well, I want to say amorphous. Sort of writhing, with no distinct body. It gave off a dark aura that frightened the life out of me. I've never seen anything like it in my life and I never want to again."

"I'm so sorry you were scared."

The woman put a reassuring hand on my arm. "It's not your fault. But…just be careful, that's all. Be very careful." Her male companion returned from paying for some postcards. "We have to go now. But remember what I said."

Her look, almost of pity, unnerved me, but I nodded and said, "Thank you," and my gaze followed them as they left the shop. I noticed how the woman leaned on her companion and it worried me.

So where did that leave me? I had always assumed my specter was there to warn me of something momentous. But now it seemed as if it might cause the momentous to happen. That turned everything on its head and all my childhood insecurities rushed to the surface.

Greg touched my shoulder, his new book now in a bag under his arm. "You don't look well, Alex. I think we'd better get you back to the guest house straightaway. You're as white as a sheet. Will you be able to walk, or shall we get a taxi?"

I needed air. "I'd rather walk, thanks. I'll feel better when we get outside. It's very claustrophobic underground. I don't know how those poor people managed."

"Me neither."

Never had bed been more inviting. At just before four, I had a good two hours before I needed to get changed and ready to go out for dinner. I laid back and my head sank into the soft pillow. Then I remembered I hadn't switched my phone back on, but my need for sleep proved stronger than my need to check my phone for messages that I was sure wouldn't even be there. Greg had gone for a walk so he wouldn't disturb me. I closed my eyes and let myself drift off.

———

"I'm sorry, love, I didn't mean to wake you."

"What time is it?" I asked, trying to focus sleep laden eyes on Greg.

"Five to six."

"Good job you did wake me. I've got to get changed, shower, slap my make up on…"

"I'm going to change my shirt," he said, laughing.

I smiled. "It's always so much easier for men."

Then I remembered my phone. I reached for my bag and retrieved it from its little pocket. I switched it on and found a voicemail. At first I thought I had a heavy breather. The wheezing wasn't punctuated with any words and I nearly deleted it when a faint voice spoke.

"You left a message…you said you were looking for a descendant of Adrian Devine…of Arnsay…" There was a long pause and then a deep, wheezing sigh. "You've found him."

The phone went dead. No hint of whether he would call back or whether I should call him. I checked the number. "Private". I couldn't call him back anyway, as he'd withheld his number.

Greg touched my arm. "Everything okay? You look puzzled."

"No, no, it's fine. Just had one of those nuisance calls, insisting I had an accident three years ago and can claim a load of money."

"Makes a change from PPI." Greg grinned.

I smiled and nodded.

In the shower, I thought about the strange message. On the plus side, I could now stop making fruitless phone calls, as I'd narrowed my search down to the nine phones on which I had left a message. On the minus side, I still didn't know exactly who he was and I couldn't make any contact with him. I would have to wait for him to call me again. If he chose to.

Or I could visit each of the nine houses in turn and find him that way. A bit stalker-ish maybe. But, after all, he had contacted me. The more I thought about it though, the prospect of knocking on strange doors appealed to me less and less. Besides, how would I explain *that* to Greg? With our car still sitting snugly in its garage four hundred miles away down south, and the addresses spread out all over Edinburgh and surrounding district, we would be talking about a full day and not inconsiderable expense, unless I struck lucky early on. I was also laying myself open to some nutter who might not even be who he claimed to be.

By the time I dried my hair, I had already reluctantly decided that I would simply have to be patient and hope he called me back promptly and, preferably, when Greg wasn't around.

Chapter Nine

Edinburgh Castle. The view is magnificent, the history exciting and bloody, and there are an awful lot of steps. You can't come to this lovely old city without immersing yourself in it, before meandering along the Golden Mile to the opposite end and the Palace of Holyroodhouse.

I tried to push all thoughts of the mysterious phone call from my mind and concentrated on soaking up centuries of Scottish history. Mel Gibson had a lot to answer for. William Wallace wasn't nearly as honorable as he portrayed him, and he certainly didn't paint his face blue—or wear a kilt. Bonnie Prince Charlie wasn't a romantic hero and, as for Mary Queen of Scots... Actually, I still felt sorry for her. Especially when the tour guide took us up to her bedroom and we saw the red stain on the wooden floor, right on the spot where her musician, David Rizzo, was done to death by her jealous husband.

"The stain never goes away," said the guide ominously.

Greg bent close to my ear. "That's because it isn't a stain at all. It's the natural color of the wood."

Another tourist gave him a furious glare.

I stifled a giggle and whispered back. "You've just shattered her illusions."

I was rewarded by another angry stare.

Feeling like a naughty schoolgirl, I made my way down the stairs. Outside, we blinked in the bright sunlight. I looked over at the ultra-modern Scottish Parliament building across the road.

"Want to go inside?" Greg asked.

I shook my head. "I'd rather have a pizza."

A gentle wander along Princes Street completed our day and I was glad to rid myself of my trainers and flex my toes.

"Expecting a call?" Greg indicated my phone. "Only you've been checking it every few minutes all day."

Had I? I hadn't been aware of it.

"No," I said as casually as I could manage before tucking the phone back in my bag.

Greg didn't seem too concerned and didn't pursue it. "I'm going to take a shower. We can go out for a drink if you like."

My aching feet didn't relish that idea. "I think I'd rather just stay here tonight. We've walked a few miles today and city streets always seem harder than anywhere else."

"Fine by me."

Greg disappeared into the bathroom and a minute later, I heard the shower.

My phone rang. I grabbed it and answered. "Hello?"

Long pause. It had to be him.

"You're looking for me, Mrs. Fletcher." It was a statement rather than a question. "You have something to say to me?"

I hesitated. His voice was gruff, wheezing. Definitely the voice of an older man— with a distinct edge to it. My fingers tingled, like pins and needles. I'd had that feeling once before...

My turn to speak. He was waiting, and I'd come this far... "Er...yes. I mean, are you related to the late Adrian Devine of Arnsay?"

A strange hissing sound, combined with more wheezing, sounded in my ear. My God, the man was laughing! My flesh crawled. If I decided to meet up with this man, I didn't want to be alone, but Greg would never go along with it.

Finally, the strange sound stopped. "You have found the right person, Mrs. Fletcher. Now, what is it you want?"

"I...need to talk to you about your...ancestor...and about Grace Devine."

Another pause.

In the bathroom, the shower stopped. Greg would be out soon.

"Come and see me tomorrow morning at eleven."

He gave me an address in Merchiston, a well-to-do suburb of Edinburgh.

I ended the call just as the bathroom door opened and Greg came out, dressed only in a large white towel.

"I heard you talking to someone," he said as he swapped the towel for a pair of boxers. "Anyone I know?"

My brain went into overdrive as I searched for a rational excuse. "Duncan from Arnsay Museum. He's been in touch with the library here and there's a possible link with the Devine family. It's great research for my novel."

"Oh. So you're going to write it then? Good. I was beginning to think you'd given up on the idea."

"Oh, I've been busy, plotting and thinking about it." I was warming to my subject now. "The Devines were really interesting and the tragedy of Grace's drowning will provide a great dramatic focus for my story."

"So you'll want to spend some time at the library then?"

"Yes. Duncan's arranged for me to see the librarian at eleven tomorrow. Is that okay with you?"

"Do you mind if I don't tag along? Not really my kind of thing and I'd probably just be in the way."

I restrained myself from rushing over to hug him and concentrated on sounding nonchalant. "No, that's fine. What will you get up to then?"

"I might go to the Academy of Art. There's a Mondrian exhibition and I know you're not all that keen."

"No, I'm not wild about him if I'm honest," I said. "We could meet back here. That way neither of us needs to rush."

―――――

I was careful to close the little wrought iron gate behind me. At the end of the short path, I stared up at the stone built, three story townhouse, took in the glossy black door, polished brass doorknob and white lace curtains at all the windows, designed to keep prying eyes out. The small front garden was neat and tidy so whoever lived here took a pride in his surroundings. For some reason, that encouraged me.

I pressed the entry buzzer and a few seconds later, the door clicked open. I pushed it wider and let myself in.

The front door opened onto a small vestibule with a glass paneled door that was closed. I turned the handle, wondering why my mouth had dried up.

A wide hallway had closed doors leading off it. I looked around. Where should I go now? An ancient grandfather clock ticked, deep and rhythmic, evoking another childhood memory. My grandmother's living room. Sunday teatime. Tea and crumpets.

I waited. Surely I would be greeted? Maybe he was arthritic and it took him time to get out of his chair?

Seconds ticked by. Five minutes past eleven.

Then I heard a scraping and a slight creak as one of the doors slowly opened. My heart thumped and I took a tentative step forward, wishing I hadn't come. Or at least not come alone.

A bent and frail-looking man swayed slightly at the entrance to the room. His sparse white hair stuck up in tufts and his suit looked straight from a 1930s film set, complete with gray and white striped waistcoat and a pocket watch on a long gold chain. My eyes traveled down his emaciated body to his shoes. In contrast with the shabby state of the rest of him, these were black patent and gleamed.

He peered at me over half-moon, wire-framed glasses.

"Mrs. Fletcher, I assume." The wheezing voice from the telephone was unmistakable.

"You assume correctly, sir. I'm Alexandra Fletcher."

I moved closer and stuck out my hand for the customary handshake. He ignored it and continued to peer at me. His bloodshot eyes were a little misted and I guessed he might have cataract problems.

"My name is Devine."

No first name then. Oh well, it didn't matter, as I wouldn't have felt comfortable using it anyway. Something about this man didn't invite familiarity.

Mr. Devine staggered a little as he retraced his faltering steps back into the room. I followed him, keeping a slight distance.

The large room was cluttered, Edwardian style, with velvet curtains in a deep burgundy hanging at four tall windows and an assortment of generously stuffed chairs in a variety of styles. Oil paintings of Scottish landscapes adorned the walls and I almost expected to see an aspidistra in a bowl on the grand piano in one corner of the room, but it was bare.

The whole place looked in need of a good dusting, but was otherwise tidy. Mr. Devine seemed fond of books. Floor to ceiling shelves lined one wall and a small, higgledy pile of leather-bound volumes leaned precariously on an occasional table next to the Chesterfield wing chair into which he now lowered himself.

He reached for a decanter of either red wine or port, positioned next to the books on the table and poured himself a generous measure, but he made no attempt to invite me to join him. Not that I would at that time; it was far too early for me. I also wasn't at all sure where the glasses would be kept, or how clean they would be.

He didn't invite me to sit down either, but I certainly wasn't going to stand any longer. I selected a nearby chair nearby and perched on the edge.

Mr. Devine took a deep sip of his drink and seemed to be sizing me up. His gaze traveled up and down my body and I had the unpleasant sensation of being violated. My imagination had gained the upper hand, of course. The man was half-blind!

I decided one of us would have to break the silence, and it might as well be me, so I cleared my throat. "Thank you for seeing me today, Mr. Devine. As I may have said in my voice message, my husband and I have been staying on the island of Arnsay and, while I was there, I came across the sad story of Grace Devine." I paused. At the mention of Grace's name, a shadow passed over the old man's face. His indeterminate expression gave way to a scowl.

"I'm sorry," I said. "Have I said something to offend you?"

A lengthy silence followed that I didn't feel able to break. The man seemed to be experiencing some kind of inner turmoil. His thin lips quivered. "You have not offended me. Carry on."

Order received, I did so. "I understand that Grace's death pretty much broke up the family. The eldest son was held responsible for her death and ordered to leave the island by his father. He was never heard from again and I'm keen to trace his descendants, so I can continue my research and find out how he lived the rest of his life."

The old man wheezed and took another deep sip of his drink. He replaced the empty glass on the table and I saw his fingers shook far more than when I had arrived.

"Adrian Devine came to Edinburgh in 1902, to make his fortune. He bought this house, married once and had a son."

"And you are that son?"

Mr. Devine nodded, slowly, his bony fingers trembling even more as he gripped the arms of his chair.

"Did your father ever speak of his time in Arnsay?"

His hands gripped the chair arms so hard, his knuckles blanched. "He never spoke of that time. Arnsay, and his family there, were dead to him." Gradually he lessened his grip and the trembling settled. "There's nothing more I can tell you, Mrs. Fletcher. Your research is over."

"Oh, no," I said and then wished I hadn't. "Could I just ask one more question? Are there any more close descendants?"

The old man's features transformed into fury. His paper-thin skin turned a vivid shade of purple and a vein throbbed at his temple.

"I am the only one left and I am asking you to leave, Mrs. Fletcher. Please leave my house and do not root around any further in matters which do not concern you."

I struggled out of the chair. "But Mr. Devine, I really don't mean any harm. I'm just so interested in your family's history."

"No, you are not. I sense a different purpose in you. You're searching for something, Mrs. Fletcher, and your dishonesty in not revealing its nature does you no credit." His voice was firmer than before. Firmer and somehow venomous. For some reason, this man had really taken against me.

"Don't make me have to ask you again, or it will go badly for you. Please leave. Now. And don't let me hear that you have been grubbing around my family's records. Do I make myself clear?"

I stared at him. What on earth had I done for him to be so rude? My instinct to retaliate at being so misunderstood nearly overwhelmed my better judgment. Fortunately, I held back. "Mr. Devine, I am very sorry indeed if I have done something to offend you. I am writing a book—"

"Not about my family you're not!" He gripped the chair arms again and seemed about to raise himself.

He was old, infirm and I could have knocked him out with one hefty blow, but at that moment, the waves of hatred that saturated the air around him, had me in retreat.

"Goodbye, Mr. Devine." I scurried to the door, opened it and raced down the hall, anxious to be out of that house as fast as I could.

I drew in lungfuls of fresh air as I ran down the short path to the gate. As I closed it behind me, I took a quick glance back at the house, certain I saw a lace curtain twitch. He was watching me, probably to ensure I really had left.

I retraced my steps back to the bus stop, but as we drove along the pleasant streets, something bugged me.

Only when I got off the bus did I realize what was wrong. The room I had been in was at the back of the house and the curtain had moved in a window at the front. Given the speed with which I'd left, the old man would have either had to develop an almighty spring in his step, or there was someone else in that house. Of course, it could be the hired help, but if so, why didn't they open the door? Was there someone else there Mr. Devine didn't want me to meet? That would explain his extreme reaction to my simple request for information.

During the short walk back to the guest house, I tried to establish what, if anything, I had gained from the traumatic meeting. The old man had stated that he was the "only one left", but how did I know if he was telling the truth? Grace needed Adrian's forgiveness and, in his absence, I had to find his closest living relative. We'd already established Duncan wouldn't do.

I needed to know if I had the right one and what the hell I was supposed to do next. As I inserted the key in the lock, my mind drifted to the painting, lying safe and hidden in the wardrobe. I had to make contact with Grace, and the painting seemed the only way to do it.

Greg was sitting on the edge of the bed, sipping a cup of coffee. He put down his newspaper and came over to plant a kiss on my cheek. "Enjoy your morning?"

Now what would I say? The library could prove a handy alibi if I played it right. More guilt. But I stuck with my story. "Fine, thanks. I'll need to go back though. There was too much to take in all at once. Do you mind?"

"Not at all. We've never been joined at the hip. Besides, I need to go back to the Academy. Like you, there was just too much to take in."

"Great. Tomorrow then and we can do something together in the afternoon."

"Right now, I'm starving. Let's grab a burger."

I wagged my finger at him. "We ate junk food yesterday. Today, we'll grab a nice, healthy salad."

"And fries." He laughed.

"Oh… all right then. And fries."

"I want to call in at reception on the way out though. I'm not at all happy about the state the cleaner left our bathroom in. Come and have a look."

Curious, I followed him.

Greg pointed to the bath. "Look at the state of that."

I slid past him and stared down at a pile of green gunge clustered around the plughole. I put my hand out.

"Oh, Alex, that's gross! You're not going to pick it up. Oh, God, you are."

He backed away as I stared, fascinated, at the trailing, weed-like substance that uncurled itself around my fingers. I had seen something just like it a few days earlier.

That time, I'd been lying on the floor of our room on Arnsay and this stuff had been clinging to my jeans. So what was lake weed doing in a guest house bathroom in the center of Edinburgh? Last time, no one but me had seen it and then only for an instant. This time was different. This time, it had involved Greg, and now I was sure I had uncovered something this morning.

Something I would live to regret.

Chapter Ten

"Please don't complain about it, Greg."

My husband stared at me as if I had just told him I was an alien.

"Why not? It's totally unacceptable to leave a bathroom in a state like that. It wasn't as bad as that *before* the cleaner came in."

"I know and that's my point."

"What?"

I sighed and tried to sort my thoughts into a logical order. I had to make him understand. "Look, Greg, don't ask me to explain it, because I can't, but the cleaner is not responsible for the state of our bathroom."

"Oh, really? Then who is? You? Me? I don't think so."

"No, look, just calm down for a moment. Ever since we arrived in Arnsay, some odd things have been happening. It's all to do with the Devine family. I learned something there that made me want to come to Edinburgh but the thing is, the weird things that happened on Arnsay are beginning to happen here too. There has to be a connection."

Greg said nothing. For a diehard skeptic like him, it would be a tough call. Finally he spoke. "Look, Alex, I'm aware you believe in a lot of stuff I can't get my head around. I know you think you see ghosts and all sorts of other stuff, but that rubbish in the bath isn't supernatural. It's pond weed or something. It didn't just appear there. Someone put it there—"

"Oh, yes? And why would a cleaner do that?"

"I've no idea."

"Don't you see? Your theory doesn't make sense!"

"So what's your theory then? Fairies dropped it perhaps, or maybe the ghost of the late—what was her name? Grace? That's it. The ghost of the late Grace Devine put it there to surprise you."

"You may not be as far off the truth as you think."

"Oh, rot!" Greg threw back the chair he had been sitting on and it overturned. He bent to retrieve it. "I'll see you downstairs. I'm going to see the manager."

I sped into the bathroom. "Well, you'll have nothing to show him."

Greg followed me, just in time to see me lift up the toilet seat, my hand clutching the weed.

"Don't do that, Alex."

I ignored him, dropped the weed in the toilet and flushed it.

"I can't believe you did that," he said.

An irrational, white-hot rage boiled inside me. "Tell you what, you can report the next load of pond weed we find."

Greg shook his head and turned away. "What's happening here, Alex?" His words extinguished the fury inside me. He sounded so sad, I just wanted to comfort and reassure him but, at that moment, my fears that he would reject me made me hang back.

He grabbed his jacket off the hook on the back of the door. "I'm going out for a walk."

"I'll join you," I said.

"No, if you don't mind, I'd rather just cool off by myself. I won't be long."

"Okay." Why argue? All this over a stupid bit of impossible weed. No way could I tell him about the strange old man and my visit to Merchiston that morning.

As the door closed behind him, I burst into tears. I sobbed for my marriage, for Greg and for myself. How could I carry on with this mission I had accepted, knowing it could wreck my entire life? I had never kept so many secrets from my husband and it gnawed at me, like a mouse chewing through wood, its sharp teeth stabbing, splintering. Anytime now, it would make a hole, big enough to crawl through.

But if I stopped, Grace would be trapped, unable to cross over, and I was so close now. I had found Adrian's son, but I needed more, and I wouldn't be welcome back in that house for reasons I couldn't understand. I didn't have time on my side either. In a few days, I would return to my own life, adjusting to redundancy, maybe actually writing that novel I said I was researching.

Then my thoughts turned to the painting. With Greg out, how many other chances might I get to be alone with it? I hated even the thought of touching it again, but it had to be done.

My legs wobbled as I stood, my eyes glued to the wardrobe, where I pictured the canvas, rolled up, buried beneath the spare blanket.

I tugged the door open, reached up and felt around. My fingers closed on the painting and I pulled it out.

Before I could think myself out of it, I slipped off the rubber band and unrolled it. A smell of dank, stagnant water hit my nostrils. Oh God, what was I going to see this time? What was it going to do to me? Drag me down into the freezing water? Pull me under so I couldn't breathe?

Every instinct screamed at me to stop, roll it up again, burn it, throw it away, anything.

Anything but go through with it.

Too late.

I stared at the young woman, motionless in the water.

"What must I do now, Grace? I've found Adrian's only son, but he threw me out of his house. And there are secrets there, secrets he doesn't want me to discover."

Nothing. Not a flicker. Minutes ticked by and still I held the picture open. Maybe if I laid it on the floor and pinned it at each corner as I had that day…

I sloughed off my shoes and knelt down, using them to anchor opposite corners. The hair dryer and my purse provided the other supports.

I leaned back on my heels and continued to stare at it. I wrinkled my nostrils at the increasingly acrid stench. Had the water become darker? Murkier? Maybe, but it could just be the quality of light in this room. I cast a quick glance at the window. The sky was overcast and no sunlight shone onto the picture.

"Grace, I need more. I need your help. I can't do this without you. Please tell me what I have to do."

I cried out as the girl's eyes flashed open—just for an instant—then closed again.

Water rushed behind me. Someone had turned the taps full on.

I scrambled to my feet and raced in. The bath was already half full. I edged forward. The hot water tap was almost scalding to the touch, but when I put my hand in the bath, I shivered. Then the water began to change color. Slowly at first, then gaining momentum, it went from clear to pale turquoise, then darkened to a deep, slimy green within seconds. The cloying, sickly sweet stench of putrefaction and rotting vegetation sent bile shooting up into my throat. I retched as I put one hand over my nose and mouth and pulled the plug out with the other. My hand came away covered in slime.

I turned to the sink and ran my hands under a rushing stream of clear, warm water. The smell disappeared as fast as it had arrived and I turned back to see the bath empty, clean, as if the past few minutes had never happened. All except for one thing.

On the white bath mat, a footprint—the outline of a small, bare foot. Too little to be mine.

Greg found me cowering on the bathroom floor. I had stared at the footprint as it gradually faded, until no trace remained, but still I couldn't move.

"Alex, what are you doing down there?"

I tore my gaze away from the mat and suddenly my vision rippled and shimmered. A furious buzzing rang in my ears.

"I...don't...I don't know. One minute I was looking at the bathmat..." I looked for it on the floor, but it no longer lay there. It hung over the bath again, just where it should have been.

With a plummeting heart, I realized Greg was holding something out to me.

"I found this on the bedroom floor. It's a painting of sorts. Not a terribly inspiring subject though. Where did you get it? I don't remember seeing it before. Did you buy it in Arnsay?"

I stared at it. God, now I would have to explain the bloody thing. Except Greg had already given me the perfect answer.

"Yes. I thought it might make a nice souvenir of our trip."

Greg laughed. "Other people buy T-shirts or tea towels. Trust you to buy the most macabre picture you could find."

I struggled to my feet. My head had cleared now and I could focus again. Mercifully the buzzing had stopped too. Greg held the painting out in front of him and I peered over at it. I blinked a few times before I would believe it.

The picture had changed. Grace no longer floated in the water; she lay on the bottom of it and she looked as if she had been there for days. Her torn and dirty dress revealed that some of her flesh had gone, devoured no doubt by the lake's hungry inhabitants, small fish, trout maybe and numerous microscopic burrowing creatures. Her fingers were part exposed bone, but wound around them, her locket gleamed dully. The sight of it, no longer around her neck where she always wore it, bothered me. Though I didn't know why.

She lay on her side and, clearly, something had been at her eyes. All that remained of the one now visible was the empty, bony eye socket. Her partially eaten nose and lips exposed part of her jawbone and teeth. Bile rushed to my throat and I swallowed hard, hating the sweet taste in my mouth. Greg let go the painting and it curled up, with a whoosh.

I allowed him to steer me back into the bedroom. "Let's get you on that bed. You're worrying me now. I really think you need to get to the hospital and let them take your blood pressure or run some tests. You're pale as a ghost."

For some reason that struck me as amusing, especially coming from the great skeptic himself. I laughed.

"I can't see anything funny, Alex. I'm serious. I don't think you're well."

The bile receded and I stopped swallowing so hard. "I'm sorry. I'm fine now. Really."

"I'd still be happier if you'd go to A and E."

"*No.*" I even startled myself with the vehemence. "No, honestly. If it happens again, then I'll go, but I'm not going to start wasting their time, or ours, on an unnecessary trip to hospital. They've enough to do there looking after people who are really sick. They don't need malingerers."

"You're hardly that."

"Maybe not, but I think the whole thing's a waste of time. If there was anything really wrong, I'd be feeling some ill effects now, wouldn't I? Well, I can assure you I'm not."

Greg's frown showed no sign of lessening, so I allowed him to pull the covers over me and settled back against the pillows.

He sat on the bed beside me and clasped my hand. "Why did you buy that awful picture? It's not as if we don't already have as many pictures as we need. Where were you going to hang it?"

I shrugged. "I've no idea. I just saw it and it's supposed to depict the drowning of Grace Devine, so I thought it would be a memento. Daft really, because you're right. There's no way I'd want to look at that all day."

Greg sighed and smiled. "Thank God for that. I thought you'd lost it there for a moment."

I smiled. Lost it? Take this week's prize for understatement, Greg. And now I'd told him yet another lie. Where was all this going to end?

My dreams that night were all of the locket. It didn't seem to matter whether I started to dream about my old job or a peaceful cornfield, sooner or later the locket made an appearance.

I woke suddenly as if I'd been dragged from my sleep. Outside, a thin gray light, tinged with pink, struggled to filter through the curtains. I peered at the bedside clock radio. Five-twenty. The dawn chorus was gaining momentum. Beside me, Greg slept on.

Careful not to disturb him, I pushed aside the covers and slipped out of bed. I found the picture where I'd put it back, in the wardrobe, and took it into the bathroom.

Once inside, I closed the door, locked it and switched on the light. A fan, mounted in the ceiling, began to whirr, mercifully quietly. It shouldn't disturb Greg.

Holding my breath, I heard my heart pounding in my ears. Would the painting have changed again? How? My fingers trembled as I unrolled it.

Surely her left arm hadn't been so skeletal? And her feet had been more flesh-covered. Now the bones stuck out. Eerily white. It looked as if another couple of weeks had gone by, or maybe deterioration happened much quicker under water? Mercifully, in her current state, she couldn't open her eyes and stare at me anymore.

I looked for the locket and found it, still entwined in her bony fingers. Had she been buried with it? Duncan had said they dragged the lake and found her body in a poor state of preservation, but he hadn't mentioned any jewelry she might have been wearing. Maybe she wanted me to find her locket and return it to her in that vault in the kirk on Arnsay. How, or when, I would do that, I hadn't a clue. I couldn't even fathom out how to get back into the old man's house.

What had I been thinking of, to take on such a formidable task as this? If only Duncan had been there. Well, after breakfast I would do the next best thing. I would phone him, tell him what I had found out so far and ask him what I should do next. Maybe he could pave the way somehow. If I gave him Mr. Devine's address and phone number, perhaps he could make contact?

Greg overslept and decided to take his shower after breakfast. While I waited for him, I called Duncan. I brought him up to date, careful to keep my voice low. He said little beyond a "Well done!" when I told him about finding Adrian's son. I still couldn't bring myself to confess to the theft of the painting, not that it even looked like the one I had stolen from the museum anymore.

"And now I'm stuck, Duncan. He threw me out of his house and I haven't fulfilled my promise to Grace. Any ideas would be really welcome because I'm running out of time."

I heard a deep sigh at the other end of the phone. "I don't know what to suggest. I'm happy to phone him, of course, but I don't know if it will do any good. It may even do harm."

"At the moment, doing nothing seems about the most harmful thing. Apart from my situation, that man isn't getting any younger. He looked as if he might drop dead any moment and he said he was the only one left. Without him…"

"Give me his number and I'll call him. Then, I'll ring you back."

Without hesitation, I gave him the number and rang off. A few minutes later, Greg emerged from the bathroom, drying his hair with a hand towel.

"Who was that?" he asked.

"The museum. They have a lead for me. They're going to call back, but I may need to go back there today. Is that okay?"

Greg pulled a face. Then relented. "No, it's fine, I'll go in search of a few bottles of single malt to take home with us."

I smiled. "And sample a few along the way, I've no doubt."

His face took on an innocent look. "Of course. How else can I know if they're any good?"

"Enjoy yourself. Just try not to get too pickled before dinner."

My phone rang. Duncan.

"Hi," I said.

"He'll see you this morning."

"How did you manage that?" I was aware of a curious look from Greg. "I mean, that's great. What time?"

"No time like the present. He said to come straight over."

Greg was still watching me, so I had to be careful.

"What was the response to your enquiry?"

"You're not alone. Right. I'll speak and you just listen. Okay? I told him who I was and how we were related. He made no comment. All I got was this constant wheezing. He sounds as if he has bronchitis or emphysema and I see what you mean about his life expectancy. Anyway, I just said that you wanted to see him again, as you had some unanswered questions, and he said, "Tell the girl to come now" and hung up."

"How…interesting," I said. "I'll be there as quickly as I can."

My brain raced to construct an explanation Greg would be satisfied with as I clicked my phone off.

"Back to the museum, I take it," Greg said, as he slipped on his shoes.

I nodded. "They've found more information about Adrian. Sounds as if it might be quite fascinating. Just what I need for my book. Bit of drama." I mentally crossed my fingers as I said that. Whatever his reason for seeing me, I hoped it wasn't overly dramatic. Mr. Devine only had to be in the same room as me to send my nerves into spasm.

On the bus going over there, I consoled myself with the thought that if all went well, this might be the last time I had to go anywhere near that house. And, if everything went exceptionally well, Grace could be at peace by the end of the day.

Just as before, the entry buzzer let me in to an empty hallway with closed doors. This time, I made my way to the room Mr. Devine had emerged from before. I hesitated before knocking. I thought my knees might buckle under me at any moment and my mouth felt like the Sahara.

From a room across the hall, I heard a scuffling, like someone shuffling across an uncarpeted floor in slippers. My hand was poised ready to knock but I hesitated again, hardly daring to breathe in case I missed something—another noise, a movement, a door opening… Seconds ticked by. Nothing. Maybe I had imagined it. Maybe they had mice?

I shook my head and knocked.

"Enter." That familiar wheezing rasp. I opened the door.

Mr. Devine wore an old-fashioned, red velvet smoking jacket and a sour expression.

"Thank you for agreeing to see me again, sir," I said and wished I could swallow, but my dry mouth wouldn't let me.

His expression didn't even flicker.

"You want something from me. What is it? As you can see, I am unwell and cannot be bothered with intrusions. Or silly young women who think they can write about whoever they like."

"I deeply regret that, Mr. Devine. I can assure you I'm not writing a book about your family. I never was—"

"So you lied to me the last time you were here?"

Anxious to justify myself, the words tumbled out. "I didn't mean to…it's just…I mean, I…I thought if told you the truth you would think I was mad."

"Truth? What truth?"

I took a deep breath. "That I've seen the ghost of Grace Devine and I need to trace the closest living relative of Adrian Devine's in order to obtain his forgiveness."

The old man lowered himself into the Chesterfield and leaned his bony hands on the arms.

The wheezing sounded like wind rushing in and out of a cave. "Forgiveness?"

"Yes, sir. Grace died with a curse on her lips. She cursed your father, and until he or—as that's impossible—his closest descendant, forgives her for that curse, she cannot pass over."

Behind me, I heard the door creak open and the old man's gaze switched from me to the new arrival.

"Who have we here then, Martyn? Our promised visitor? You should have told me. I would have been here to greet her myself."

I spun around to face a tall, middle-aged man, dressed in the sort of suit I had seen in Victorian photographs. The sort Jonas Devine would wear. In fact, his face bore a striking resemblance to Jonas's.

He extended his hand towards me.

"Good morning, Mrs. Fletcher. I believe you have been looking for me. My name's Adrian Devine."

Chapter Eleven

His firm, dry handshake was that of a confident man. I noticed he had thin lips and, although he was smiling, the expression never extended to his eyes. They were cold and almost black. Now I could see it. He had the look of a gypsy, his face little changed from the photograph of the young boy I had seen. But he *couldn't* be the same Adrian Devine, could he?

"Pleased to meet you, Mr. Devine."

He let his hand fall. "Adrian please, if we are to be friends. And we are, aren't we, Alexandra?"

I was glad he hadn't called me 'Alex'. I would have been uneasy with such familiarity from this disturbing man. And he'd called himself Adrian. Coincidence surely?

I croaked, then cleared my throat. "Forgive me for asking, but I'm trying to work out the relationship here. It's really important I find the closest living descendant I can to the Adrian Devine who was stepbrother to Grace when they lived on the island of Arnsay at the turn of the last century."

Adrian motioned me to sit and I perched on the edge of the same chair as on my previous visit. Then he moved to the mantelpiece and opened a small wooden box. He removed a long, thin cigar and lit it with a lighter he took out of his pocket. A momentary, distinctive smell of petrol wafted over to me as he struck the flint and the flame shot three inches upwards. He puffed a few times, then shut the lighter with a sharp metallic snap. He waved the cigar at me.

"You don't mind, do you? Dreadful habit I know, but I can't seem to shift it."

As a lifelong non-smoker, I can't say I'm wild about passive smoking, but it was his own house. Or the old man's. Just what relationship did these two men share?

Martyn Devine shifted in his seat. His arthritis or rheumatism must be playing him up. I saw Adrian pick it up too.

"You can leave us now. Go and rest."

I would love to have said his voice held compassion for the older man, but Adrian Devine had issued an order and was clearly used to being obeyed. Right now, I just wanted this meeting over, so I could escape too. No words were spoken as the old man shuffled to the door, opened it and then closed it quietly behind him.

In the silence, I thought back to the shuffling I had heard as I had been about to knock. It belonged much more to the man who had just left than the man who had entered. Was anything going to make sense today?

"Now, Alexandra, what can I do for you?"

I sensed he already knew why I was there. So, why ask? I pushed the unwelcome thought aside. "Are you Adrian Devine's closest living relation?"

I don't know what reaction I expected — certainly not amusement. But Adrian Devine threw back his head and laughed, revealing perfect white teeth. Then he seemed to register my expression, which must have reflected at least a little of the shock I felt.

"Oh, I do apologize. Yes, you have found the right person."

"But the other Mr. Devine, the gentleman who just left us, told me he was the only one left."

Adrian took a deep puff of his cigar and exhaled a cloud of purplish smoke, so sickly sweet I nearly gagged. I disguised the reaction as a cough.

No amusement now as Adrian's voice became low and serious. "He becomes confused at times. He is very old, you know."

"Is he your father? If so, he must be the person I need to see."

"I can assure you that he is not my father. I am the person you are seeking."

"Then who is—"

"Alexandra, you have clearly come here for a purpose and if you tell me what that is, maybe I can help or maybe I can't, but we'll never know unless you tell me."

The edge to his voice—like a knife slicing through paper. All I wanted to do right then was get out of there, but I didn't, God help me. I pushed my fear aside and stayed.

He waited for my response, tapping manicured nails on the occasional table next to his chair.

I swallowed hard. "I'm sorry, but it's difficult to know where to begin. How much do you know about your family on Arnsay?"

The tapping stopped. He stubbed out his cigar and threw it into the empty fireplace. "Enough."

"And do you know what happened on January 24th, 1902, the day Grace Devine drowned in the lake?"

"Yes."

So far, so good, but the next part would call for a giant leap of faith. I licked dry lips. "This next question is going to seem very strange and I apologize, but I have to know. Do you believe in the supernatural, Mr. Devine?"

The man opposite me exhaled. His face was expressionless and I had no idea what was going on behind those dark eyes beyond an impression that they were somehow growing larger.

I didn't see him move one step nearer, but he grew, until he filled my field of vision. My eyes wouldn't stay open and I drifted, as if I was sinking, deeper and deeper into the chair, further and further back.

I heard his voice, but couldn't make out any words, just a soporific wave of sound that soothed and calmed me. Echoes of voices swept past me and I floated on a calm sea. Was I asleep? Dreaming maybe? Perhaps. As I drifted, nothing mattered. All sense of time and distance were lost. I didn't even know if I was still in my body.

A clock chimed. I counted one, two, three, four. Nothing. I opened my eyes. I was still in the same room, alone and lying on a velvet-covered chaise longue. The colors in the room seemed more vibrant somehow.

Afternoon sunlight poured in and I looked down at myself. Instead of my dark blue jeans, T-shirt and trainers, I saw, to my amazement, I was dressed in a lilac, ankle-length dress and black, button boots. Instinctively, I put my hand up to my head and, instead of my straight, loose hair, I was met with waves and hairclips.

I stood and winced as the boots pinched my toes and my tight clothes restricted my breathing. In the mirror over the mantelpiece, the woman who stared back, while recognizably me, reminded me of an old Edwardian photograph.

I clapped my hand to my mouth to stifle a scream just as the door opened and a young maid brought in a tea tray.

"Had a nice nap then, madam?" She laid the silver tray down carefully on a cloth-covered occasional table. She hovered, her hand by the china teapot. "Shall I pour, madam?"

I didn't trust myself to speak, so nodded. Who on earth did she think I was? Who was she? What had happened to me? Was I still out of it?

I clasped my hands together, reassured slightly by the familiar feel of my flesh. Then I realized, I shouldn't be able to feel it, and I certainly shouldn't be able to smell the fragrant tea. Not if I was in a dream.

"Will madam be dining in this evening? Only Cook asked me to find out."

I stared at her expectant face. Her voice held a noticeable Scottish accent, and she wore a black, ankle-length dress, with boots, a crisp white apron and matching cap. A frown creased her forehead and I knew I would have to say something, however surreal this situation.

"I'm not really sure…I'm not feeling very well at the moment…"

"Oh, I'm sorry, madam. Would you like to lie down perhaps?"

"No, that's fine. It's a headache. Maybe a cup of tea will help."

The girl smiled, apparently satisfied with my explanation. I remembered from my history lessons at school, Victorian and Edwardian women frequently suffered from headaches and, indeed, fainting. As a searing pain stabbed me under my breasts and added to the discomfort of only being able to take shallow breaths, I knew why. My straitjacket of a corset was constricting my breathing.

I couldn't have dressed myself like this. Someone must have done it. But who? The girl who brought my tea? Or maybe I had a personal lady's maid. And where—or more accurately—*when* was I?

I hobbled over to the chair nearest the table and lowered myself down, certain that, at any moment, I would hear a rip as some undergarment, or even my dress, tore.

A sudden thought. Greg. He would be worried. If not now, then very soon. I must call him.

I looked around, but couldn't see my handbag and, without that, I had no phone. What was I thinking? If I had somehow slipped back in time, there would be no cell phone. And no Greg either. Tears pricked my eyelids.

"Oh, madam, you do look poorly. Can I get you anything? Some laudanum perhaps?"

Laudanum! "No, no, I'm sure it will lift. I'll just sit here quietly and sip my tea. Thank you." I wanted to ask her name. In fact I had a hundred or more questions I wanted to ask and daren't ask any of them. Not until I'd grasped whatever was happening here.

The maid bobbed a slight curtsey and left me alone with my confused and panicked thoughts. Thinking the tea might help to calm me, I added two cubes of sugar from a small silver bowl and a splash of milk. Some tiny triangular sandwiches, their crusts removed, were arranged neatly on one tea plate and two dainty sponge cakes failed to tempt me from another. Food was the last thing on my mind and, anyway, I wondered how Edwardian women managed to eat more than a morsel in these corsets. My insides felt as if they were being crushed from all directions.

I hoisted myself to my feet, limped over to the mantelpiece again and scanned the ornaments. They told me little of any use. Tiny Grecian-style vases, two ornate silver candlesticks, the chiming clock… Then I saw an envelope. I snatched it up and peered at the postmark.

April 13th 1912. So, I was right about the Edwardian era. I had no way of knowing how long the letter had been up there, of course, but, as it was the only one, and I assumed from the lack of dust that the servants did their jobs properly, I guessed it had been placed there within the last twenty-four hours.

The addressee was Mr. A. Devine, who had clearly read the contents. Never in my life had I ever gone through another person's mail, but this time I made an exception. Somehow, it seemed I really had slipped through time to his house more than a hundred years previously. Surely that wasn't by chance? Maybe this was the only way to help Grace pass over, but I hadn't the first idea how. Perhaps there might be some clue in the letter?

One small folded sheet of paper sat in my hand. The letter consisted of a few lines on one side only. The handwriting was erratic, as if written by someone in a furious temper, and the venom virtually dripped off the page:

> *Adrian,*
>
> *I have repeatedly informed you that I have no wish or desire to communicate with you. Your pathetic attempts to ingratiate yourself with me, in order to ensure your reinstatement in my Will, are futile. That you are doing well and making money come as no surprise to me. I am sure there are many broken backs lying in your wake.*
>
> *There will be no further communications from me, so it is pointless in continuing to send letters.*
>
> *May God have mercy on your blackened soul.*
>
> *Jonas Devine*

So Duncan had been wrong. There had been letters, but Jonas would have destroyed them all and probably never told Robert about any of them.

I heard footsteps coming closer and hastily stuffed the letter back in its envelope, taking care to replace it precisely where I had found it.

The door flew open and I came face to face with Adrian Devine. I gasped. He looked identical to the man I had been speaking to in my own time. Not only that, I would swear he wore the same suit.

"Mr. Devine, I..." What could I say to him? Would this Adrian Devine recognize me?

"Charlotte, my dear, what a way to address your husband."

I couldn't move. "My *what*? And who's Charlotte?"

He strode over and planted a light kiss on my cheek. Suddenly I ached for Greg.

"I don't understand…" I said as tears flooded my eyes.

"Of course not. Why would you? Now, my dear, all you need to remember is that you are my wife. We have been married for two years. We have one child, a one-year-old boy, who is largely taken care of by a most capable young nanny—"

"No, no. This isn't happening." Hysteria sent my voice up a scale. "What have you done? Why am I here?"

He attempted to put his arms around me but I shrugged him off, disgusted by his touch.

"I'll call Sarah and she can give you some laudanum. It'll calm you." He reached for the bell pull.

"You will do no such thing!" I don't know how I dared defy him, and the look on his face made me cringe, but if he thought he was going to feed me opium, he'd better think again.

I wished I could steady my heart rate and control my breathing. "I don't know how you've done this. But I don't belong here. The servants can't possibly know me because I've never seen them before in my life. For some reason you've staged all this and I don't know why. Maybe you have a warped sense of humor, who knows? But I demand you stop it right now. This is kidnapping and you are breaking the law."

As I spoke, another explanation presented itself. There was no timeslip—he had staged it because he wanted to scare me, for some reason. In reality, I was exactly where I had always been, in his house, but in 2014, not 1912. He must have drugged me, or hypnotized me somehow. Hell, if the illusionist, Derren Brown, could convince someone they had woken up in post-apocalyptic Britain, surely *this* would be easy in the hands of a professional.

Adrian Devine stared at me and I remembered how his eyes had seemed to grow larger, right before I slipped into some kind of semi-conscious, even unconscious state. Yes, that must be how he'd done it. I mustn't look at his eyes. I turned my gaze away and concentrated on the door behind him. Satisfied that I'd found the solution, I wondered briefly who had laced me into this corset and trussed me up like a Christmas turkey. Probably the maid. I couldn't think that this man would waste his time tugging at underwear. Certainly not to fasten it up at any rate.

"Charlotte, you are quite hysterical and I can do nothing with you until you have calmed down." Horrified, I watched him tug the bell pull. Well, let him summon the maid. That still didn't mean I would drink any of the poisonous stuff.

"You will take your medicine and then we will talk."

The maid appeared and bobbed her curtsey to both of us.

"Fetch madam's laudanum," he said.

"Yes, sir." She flashed me one quick glance and darted out. Was that sympathy in her eyes? I dismissed the thought. I'd already decided that she was an actress, employed by this man for this role.

Before I could collect my thoughts and make another attempt at getting the truth out of Adrian Devine, she was back.

She advanced towards me and clearly intended to give the bottle to me. I was equally determined to drop it, where I hoped it would smash, especially if I threw it at the fireplace. Adrian seemed to sense what I had in mind.

"Give it to me," he said.

The maid hesitated for a second, then turned and handed it to him.

"That will be all, Sarah."

Alone with him, I stared at the bottle in his hand. Surely he wouldn't use force to make me drink it? I watched as he measured out six drops into a small glass. He added a small measure of, what looked like brandy, from a decanter and handed the glass to me.

"I am asking you once, and only once, to drink this."

"And if I refuse?"

"That would not be advisable. Because one way or another, you are going to drink it."

I could knock it out of his hand, but there was more where that had come from. Maybe I could pretend to drink it, and then stage a choking fit and spit it out. But he'd just give me another dose.

"Drink it!"

Courage, or madness, welled up from somewhere and I slowly shook my head.

In an instant, he was behind me, his arm around my neck and the glass pressed against my lips. I struggled but he tightened his grip, until he was choking me, cutting off the air supply to my windpipe. I clamped my jaws shut, but everything started to go black as my brain was starved of oxygen. Still I struggled, but grew weaker by the second. My arms flailed helplessly at my sides and just as I was about to lose consciousness, my lips parted. The bitter liquid poured into my mouth, its foul taste only barely concealed by the brandy. He lessened his grip, but tilted my head farther back until I was sure my neck would snap. The vile stuff dripped down my throat. Then, he released me as I choked and spluttered.

He handed me his handkerchief and I wiped my mouth. Hopefully I had spat out some of the stuff, but already a warm, soothing lethargy swarmed over my body. I staggered to the chaise longue and sank down on it, barely noticing the tight clothes. Adrian pushed me back on the cushions where I'd found myself when I first came to in this pseudo-world.

His face swam in front of my eyes as a drug-induced euphoria took hold of me. I no longer cared where I was, or whether I was part of this man's warped fantasy world. He smiled at me, or was that the laudanum as well?

He moved a chair closer to me, sat down and leaned forward. "Now we will talk."

I floated in and out of consciousness. Never in my life had I experienced such tranquility, in mind and body. It didn't matter that nothing made sense anymore. All that mattered was that I didn't care — and I liked not caring. If I didn't care, I didn't have to do anything. I could stop feeling responsible for Grace, or anything else, for that matter.

Adrian's voice drifted in and out, his words making little or no sense. Finally, my comfortable blanket of harmony closed in on me and, as I slipped away, I managed one word. "Forgiveness."

I opened my eyes, expecting to see the walls of the guest house bedroom, and it took a moment to clear my fuzzy head and realize I was still in that room in that house in Merchiston. I lay on the chaise longue and, as I moved, the boned corset dug into my flesh.

Thoughts of Greg flashed into my mind. He would be worried sick. Probably had the police out looking for me by now. I *must* call him. I looked around. Still no sign of my bag, and no telephone in sight either.

I hung on to the arm of the chaise longue as I tried to stand. My legs felt as if they belonged to someone else and a dull ache throbbed at my temples, no doubt the aftereffects of the opiate I had been given. I was alone in the room again and the clock struck. I peered over at it. Eleven-fifteen on a gray April morning.

I swayed as I made my way to the mirror to check my appearance. My hung-over face stared back at me, dark shadows under my eyes, which gave me a haunted look.

Coffee. I needed strong coffee and lots of it. The bell pull was on the right of the fireplace. What the hell? If this charade was being inflicted on me for God alone knew what purpose, I might as well derive some benefit out of it, so I pulled the cord.

The door opened within seconds. Sarah scurried in and bobbed her usual neat curtsey.

"Yes, madam?"

"A pot of coffee please, Sarah."

"Certainly, madam."

A few minutes later, the strong, restoring liquid began to work its magic. I had added a couple of spoons of sugar, and sure enough, my age old remedy worked. The headache, which had been threatening to turn into a migraine, started to lift. I looked down at my rumpled dress. I felt dirty and needed to change. Somewhere in this house, there must be a room with closets and clothes. Maybe I could find something loose to wear so I wouldn't have to tolerate the suffocating corset. I might then actually feel like eating something.

I drained my third cup of coffee, made my painful way to the door and opened it.

Sarah was dusting in the hall.

"Can I help you, madam?"

"I need to take a bath and change my clothes."

"Very good, madam. I'll send Iris to you."

I was left standing, awkwardly in the hall. Should I go up? I had no idea where to go, but at least I could have a look around.

I picked up my skirts and started to climb the stairs, but had only managed three when I heard the tapping of boots on tiles and looked down. A thin, short girl in a maid's uniform looked up at me.

"Sorry, madam. I'll go and draw your bath now."

I stood aside to let her pass and noted the curious expression on her face. Of course, if all this had been real, I wouldn't have stood aside for her at all. She was the servant. I was the lady of the house. Hierarchy mattered in those days. Whoever she was, she'd researched her role well.

She led me into a sunny room, all lemon and white, with tall windows and a comfortable-looking double bed. A large wardrobe covered most of one wall. Iris disappeared behind a door and, soon, I heard the welcome sound of running water.

I fumbled with the buttons on my dress but hadn't managed to unfasten many when the maid came out of the bathroom.

"I'll help you with that, madam."

She had obviously done this many times before, as her deft fingers soon had the hooks and eyes separated and the buttons unfastened. Then I stepped out of an assortment of underwear, including the dreaded corset. Once unlaced, the relief of being able to take a full, deep breath cleansed and refreshed me. Just in that one small gesture, I began to feel more alive.

I stared at the corset, slung over the bedstead. Never again!

Iris draped a floor-length robe around my shoulders and I tied the sash around my waist.

"Thanks, Iris. I can take it from here," I said.

"Very good, madam. Shall I lay out your primrose for the afternoon?"

Not knowing what 'my primrose' was, I couldn't say. "No, that's fine. I'll decide what to wear after I've had my bath. That's all for now, thank you."

I felt as if I was in an episode of *Downton Abbey*. Iris opened the door to leave when I thought of something. "Iris, is Mr. Devine in?"

"No, madam. I believe he had an appointment with his tailor this morning, but he should be home for luncheon."

"Just one other question; did you audition for this part, or were you personally selected?"

The girl frowned. Oh yes, she could certainly act. That look of confusion was perfect. "I'm sorry, madam, I don't understand what you mean."

"You *are* an actress, aren't you?"

I don't know what I expected her to say. After all, she could hardly admit it or she'd lose this job and no doubt, owing to its nature, she was being well paid.

She stared at me as if I'd just accused her of stealing the crown jewels. Tears filled her eyes. "I...I...really don't understand. I've been your personal maid for a year now and you always said I gave satisfaction."

We stared at each other and I knew there was no point in continuing to question her. "Thank you, Iris, that will be all," I said and turned towards the bathroom. The door closed quietly behind me.

The warm water soothed and refreshed me, gently bathing the red corset welts under my breasts. I lay there and stared at the ceiling, as I tried to make sense of my surroundings.

What did Adrian Devine want from me? And how could he even be Adrian Devine? Was the old man—Martyn—playing some kind of macabre game with me to scare me off? When Duncan called him, maybe he realized I wasn't just going to give up my research, so he decided to frighten me off for good. Pretty bizarre though.

And then there was Greg. At the thought of my husband, a tear trickled down my cheek. If only I could contact him. As soon as Adrian—or whoever he really was— returned, I would tackle him about it. Somehow or other I would get outside, find a phone and call him, reversed charges. Then I realized. You can't make reversed charge calls to cell phones and I hadn't a clue what the number was for the guest house. Of course, I could always dial 999. After all, I had been kidnapped.

Decision made, I hoisted myself out of the bath and dried myself quickly on the soft towel. My wet hair flopped around my shoulders. I couldn't imagine they'd been sloppy enough to leave a 21st century hair dryer in any of the drawers, so I towel-dried it as much as possible.

Back in the bedroom, I opened the closet doors. The rails were full of elegant gowns, neatly arranged. I went from one to the next, until I found one I could get into without the damned corset.

I dressed quickly and selected shoes I could easily slip my feet into, brushed my hair and then took a deep breath.

Outside in the hallway, I didn't hear a sound. As silently as I could, I made my way down the stairs and headed for the front door. I was nearly there, when it opened and Adrian walked in. He seemed surprised to see me.

"You look… different," he said. "Ah yes, your hair. Isn't Iris going to style it for you today?"

How long did he intend to keep this up? "Look, Adrian, or whatever your name is, I don't know how long you intend to carry on this charade, but I want to leave. Right now. Give me back my own clothes and my handbag. I need to phone my husband and let him know where I am." I would be in for an argument with Greg for my recklessness in coming here in the first place, but right now, anything was preferable to remaining one more minute in this house with this madman.

"Not in the hall, Charlotte, if you please. We don't want to add to the servants' gossip, do we?"

"Stop calling me that! My name's Alexandra Fletcher."

He pushed past me and made for the door. "In here, please. Now."

I followed him. He closed the door.

"Well?" I said.

"Dear me, you are in a state, aren't you?"

"Wouldn't *you* be? How would you feel if someone kidnapped you, drugged you and, when you woke up, tried to convince you that you'd been transported back a hundred years? It's *why* it's being done I don't understand. I came here to fulfill a promise I made to someone who was deeply wronged by Adrian Devine and, for some reason or another, his son has hired actors and created 1912 World in this house to trick me."

Adrian reached into his pocket and withdrew a silver cigarette case. He then opened it and took out a black cigarette with a gold foil tip.

"I don't smoke and I'd rather you didn't in my presence," I said.

He seemed to consider this for a moment. Then he gave a slight smile and an almost imperceptible nod, before replacing the cigarette back in its case which he then tucked into his jacket pocket.

"Feisty as ever, my dear," he said.

"Oh, come on! We don't even know each other."

"On the contrary, we've been married for two years and I've known you for five."

That did it. My hands balled into fists at my sides.

He watched me, his expression amused if anything. That just made me angrier.

"Stop this farce right *now*. I am *not* your wife. I never met you before yesterday.

What the hell is all this about?"

"If you'll sit down, I shall explain it to you. First, I need something from the bureau." He moved away to the other side of the room.

"You can get my bag while you're there," I said, adrenalin still rushing through me and giving me the courage to challenge this man.

He ignored me and came back with a photograph album.

"Sit over there, please," he said.

Anxious to get answers to my questions, I obeyed, and sat on the edge of the chaise longue.

He sat beside me, a little too close for my liking. I squirmed away, but was right on the edge, so his body still touched mine. A million tiny caterpillars crawled across my skin.

He opened the album and pointed to a photograph. He, and a woman I did not recognize, stared back at me. Taken on their wedding day, they were surrounded by, what I assumed to be, family and friends. The photograph was old-fashioned, sepia and everyone was in Edwardian clothes. Another mock up.

"Who's she then?" I asked.

He didn't answer, but turned the page instead. The young bride I had just seen, stared back from a portrait that looked as if it had been hand tinted in soft, flattering colors. As he turned page after page, he and this woman were featured, either together or separately. Sometimes she appeared with two older people I took to be her parents. Finally, he showed me half a dozen photographs where she held a baby in a long white gown.

"Our son," he said and then closed the album.

"You still haven't told me who she is and you haven't answered any of my questions." I wondered why panic was creeping up my spine. It chilled me and raised the hairs on the back of my neck.

"Haven't you guessed yet? Haven't you worked it out?"

"What do you mean?"

"The girl is you. Don't you recognize yourself?"

I stared at him. What new nonsense was this? If it wasn't so serious, it would be laughable.

"Don't be ridiculous. She doesn't look a bit like me. She had blonde hair and she's married to you, which I'm not. You're delusional if you think I'm her. Only, of course, we both know you're not and this is some elaborate scheme or prank, which has to stop *now*. It isn't remotely funny and, I will remind you, that you are holding me here against my will. You *have* to let me go."

He paused. "Come with me."

He gripped my hand and half-dragged me off the chair. I stood in front of the mantelpiece mirror.

"Look at yourself," he said.

My familiar image stared back at me, my cheeks a little flushed and my hair, still damp and untidy.

"What are you trying to prove?" I said. "As you can see, I look nothing like her."

He held up an object. A hand mirror, of the sort that came as part of an old style dressing table set.

"Now look at your reflection in the mirror through this."

Look at the reflection of my reflection? That was how you were supposed to see yourself as others see you. I twisted my head, until my image came into view. Reflection of my reflection.

Except it wasn't me. Staring back at me was the girl in the album, but she wore the same green dress as me and her blonde hair lay in damp curls around her shoulders.

I gasped.

"Now do you believe me?" he asked as an unpleasant smile twisted his lips.

My eyes filled up and in the reflection, tears streamed down the blonde girl's cheeks.

Chapter Twelve

I sank down on the chaise longue, too scared and confused to speak. But Adrian—I supposed I must call him that now—hadn't finished with me yet.

"Do you still think this is an elaborate hoax? That our servants are actors and that this is not 1912? Come with me and I will prove it to you."

I let him lead me into the hall. He opened the front door and, straightaway, I heard the clattering of horses' hooves, the racket of carriages and early cars, hooters honking.

Adrian linked my arm in his, and marched me down the path and onto the pavement. By now, the sounds of a newspaper vendor, announcing the latest edition, and a hurdy-gurdy man had joined the melee. Pungent fumes from the exhausts of cars and horse manure filled the air.

I walked like an automaton, too stunned to speak or protest. Men in tails and top hats passed us. Ladies dressed in smart, stylish Edwardian coats and hats cast me curious glances. By their standards, I must look a state, with no coat or hat, and my hair loose and untidy.

At the corner, the newspaper seller turned out to be a young boy of no more than twelve. Adrian handed over a coin and, as the boy passed him a newspaper, I read the headline: "Titanic Sunk. Great Loss of Life." I saw the date: April 16th 1912.

My hands trembled and a little whimper escaped my lips.

I gazed around wildly, earning more disapproving stares, but I didn't care. I was no longer in my world. This was an alien place, with alien people. How had I come here? How could I escape back to my own world, my own time—and Greg?

"Come along, my dear, people are staring. Let me get you back home."

I didn't protest. I just did as I was told. After all, he knew how to behave in this world, whereas I hadn't a clue.

I felt almost relieved to be back in the relatively familiar surroundings of his house. Half an hour later, I attempted to eat Sole Veronique, but only managed a couple of mouthfuls. I hadn't spoken one word since our return.

Adrian sat at the far end of the dinner table. He pushed his empty plate away, leaned back in his chair and patted his lips with his napkin. I watched him take a large swig of water.

He cleared his throat. "I think it best if we tell everyone you are unwell, until you have had chance to get used to the situation. We can say you have a touch of fever. The servants are very discreet. They will say nothing."

"Do you know what's happened to me? Can you remember meeting me in this house in 2014?"

He pushed his chair back and went over to the window. Eventually he spoke. "No, Charlotte, that didn't happen. I will tell you the truth of what happened. You were born Charlotte Fitzgerald here, in Edinburgh, in 1882. Your parents are Matthew and Mary Fitzgerald. Your father and I were business associates for a time, until he made a very serious mistake, which resulted in the loss of many thousands of pounds. He faced ruin. If I had pressed charges, he could have been convicted of fraud, but I didn't. I made a deal with him. A deal, I might add, he had no hesitation in accepting—my silence, in return for your hand in marriage."

I let the words sink in. "You...*bought*...me?"

"Oh, hardly bought, my dear. No, I exchanged you. That way, we were all happy."

"You bought me," I said, as if repeating it would make it somehow less disgraceful. And who was this dreadful father who would sell his own daughter like a prostitute, to settle some debt? As for happy, I doubted that. The mere thought of Adrian's hands on me made me want to vomit and I was determined he wouldn't get me in his bed. Now I had to accept he really *was* Adrian Devine, I also had to accept that I was living with Grace's killer.

My eyes filled with tears and I sobbed for my lost life. Friends. The films I would never see now, the books I wouldn't read because their authors hadn't even been born yet. I wept for the technology I took for granted and the independence I wouldn't now have. Hell, as a woman in this world, I couldn't even vote!

But these thoughts were nothing compared to the overwhelming loss of Greg. I ached to see him again, to touch him, stroke his face, run my fingers through his hair, hold him in my arms. Every thought was torture and, while I sobbed my heart out, Adrian Devine, the man who now claimed to be my husband, stood and watched. Not one hint of concern or sympathy in his face. He might even have enjoyed the spectacle.

"What part have you played in this?" My voice cracked, but he couldn't mistake my fury.

He spread his hands. "I can assure you, I have no idea what you're talking about."

"You most certainly do! I came to see the old man, and you came in. Then I found myself back here. You can't deny that happened. I was there. And so were you. You made this happen and I want to know why."

He grabbed my hands but I resisted and pushed him away. His face grew flushed and angry.

"I don't know what ails you, but I will not have this defiance in my own home. Now either you stop this nonsense and behave as a respectable and dutiful wife to me, or I shall be forced to summon the doctor and have him prescribe some calming tonic."

More laudanum! That bloody stuff had kept more than one generation of women docile, until they woke up and realized what was happening.

"I *won't* take it."

He laughed. "If I say you'll take it, you will take it. Remember what happened yesterday."

I glared at him, my anger all the greater because I knew he was right. He had me just where he wanted me. The more I resisted, the more entrenched he would become and then I would never be able to persuade him to forgive Grace. Besides, he must be doing all right financially. I didn't know what the curse was, but it didn't seem to have done him much harm.

Cornered, I decided my best weapon was to play the agreeable, acquiescent wife. At least for now. If I could lull him into a sense of false security, maybe he would grow more malleable, or let his guard slip.

"That's better." He sounded as if he was talking to a pet lapdog. "Now you've calmed down, why don't you ask Iris to style your hair and dress you more appropriately? You look slovenly."

I nodded and hurried out of the room.

Once upstairs, I rang for my maid. She appeared within a minute.

Needless to say, the much-hated corset returned, although I did manage to dissuade her from squeezing all the breath out of my lungs.

I gasped. "I really don't need an eighteen-inch waist, Iris." She let it out as I exhaled. "Thank you, that's much better."

"Yes, madam." I caught the merest hint of disapproval, but ignored it. If I had to live in these times, at least for now, I didn't have to obey all their orders.

Iris had selected a pretty, emerald-green, cotton day dress with a high, lace neck.

"Would you like to wear your locket with that, madam?"

Locket? Oh well, why not? "Yes, that'll be fine."

Iris took a tiny key from a glass pot on the dressing table and opened a black lacquered Japanese box. Inside were various trays and compartments and she selected an item from one of them. As I stared at my reflection in the mirror, I wondered which of us she saw—the real me, with my dark hair and brown eyes, or the blonde wife of Adrian Devine.

Then all idle thoughts crashed to a halt. She held it in front of me, ready to fasten it around my neck. I snatched it from her. "Where did you get this locket?"

The girl's face blanched and her eyes grew wide. "I—it's yours, madam. You told me the master gave it to you on your wedding day."

"He, *what*?" I turned the locket over in my hand and snapped it open. A photograph of Adrian stared out at me. I snapped it shut again and felt the cold silver. So cold, it burned my fingers. I threw it onto the dressing table and turned my hand over.

Iris gasped. "Oh, madam, your fingers!" Iris grabbed them between her own and turned her shocked eyes to mine.

"Madam, your fingers are frozen. It's as if you've plunged them into ice cold water. Whatever can be the matter? Shall I call the doctor?"

I shook my head, too horrified to speak. Impossible though it was, I had just held Grace's locket. The touch of it had turned my fingers blue with cold and they dripped icy water. "I'll be all right, Iris, but please put that locket away. I won't be wearing it again."

My fingers throbbed as the circulation flowed back into them. I rubbed them and watched Iris pick up the locket with two trembling fingers and then drop it back into the box, which she locked immediately. She didn't seem to have suffered any ill effects and she said little as she tucked in a few stray strands of my hair.

After my earlier accusations and then this, I wondered what she must think of me. Or maybe Charlotte had always behaved oddly.

Soon after, Iris left me alone and I stared at the jewelry box. I took out the key and turned it in the lock.

Adrian's wife—I couldn't begin to identify myself with that role—had amassed some lovely pieces. I presumed the stones were real and, if so, she possessed emerald necklaces and matching drop earrings, a gorgeous sapphire and diamond bracelet, and a diamond cluster that could well have been her engagement ring. All I had on my fingers was a plain gold wedding band and, when I looked closely, I realized even that didn't belong to me. Not the real me at any rate.

A massive lump formed in my throat and I swallowed with difficulty. An image of a smiling Greg flashed through my mind, along with a strong urge to curl up in a corner and sob my heart out yet again.

But I had work to do. If I was ever to see Greg again, I had to follow this through.

I searched the compartments until I found the locket. I pinched the chain between my right thumb and forefinger and dragged it out. I didn't want to touch it any more than strictly necessary, so I lay it down on the dressing table and stared at it. Nothing happened. Did I really think it would?

I touched the locket with the tip of my finger, expecting to recoil from the chill, but felt nothing; the metal felt neither cold nor hot. I worked up a little more bravery and pressed my finger against it. Nothing. I picked it up. It felt cool, but not unnaturally so.

I flicked it open again. In the photograph, Adrian was standing facing left. I fingered the empty oval frame on the right.

Behind me someone sighed.

I spun around, still holding the locket, as the door swung shut. I dashed across the room and flung it open. No one in the hall. All the other doors were shut, but whoever had been there couldn't have gone far. I crossed over to the opposite side and tried the first door handle. Locked. I listened at the door. Silence.

I repeated this four times. Two of the doors opened onto empty, furnished bedrooms. One was the bathroom. That left just one more door. I leaned against it and listened. Voices. I couldn't hear what they were saying but one was unmistakably Adrian's, the other, a woman.

My instinct was to throw open the door and surprise them. In flagrante perhaps? But instead I bent down and peered through the keyhole. I could see nothing, so the key must be in the other side, but I could hear more clearly here. The woman's voice was deep and accented. Not British. European perhaps.

She and Adrian were having a heated argument about something. I stood up and gently turned the handle. It gave and I opened the door a crack.

"I have seen it, Adrian. I have seen what will come for you," the woman said. "She put the curse on you and, if you allow her, she will haunt you all your days. Death will be a blessing for you."

"Nonsense! You removed the curse and gave me wealth and position. Nothing can destroy me now. I—"

"But she has cursed you for all eternity. Only I can protect you. Now your soul is joined with mine, you will be safe, as long as you don't let her in."

Footsteps approached. I let go the door handle and retreated, hoping to appear as if I had just come out of my room.

The door opened. Adrian gave me an irritated look as if he had just caught a child putting its hand in the cookie jar.

"Do you require something?"

"You have company?"

"Company?"

"As I was passing your room, I heard voices."

He studied me for a moment and then flung his door wide. "Come, see for yourself. There is no one here but me."

I was reluctant to enter his room, but I needed to satisfy my curiosity.

As I stepped over the threshold, I took in the heavy mahogany furniture, a typical gentleman's bedroom of the period. The bed was neatly made up and the curtains let in the afternoon sun, pale and watery after a rain shower. The room was empty. Where was she hiding?

"Perhaps you were speaking on the telephone."

"We do not yet possess such an instrument in this house, as you well know."

I resisted the temptation to issue some sarcastic reply and forced myself to lower my eyes in, what I hoped was, a demure expression. "I'm sorry, Adrian, I must have been mistaken."

"I suggest you go and visit our son in the nursery. You haven't seen him these past two days. He'll forget who his mother is."

"Perhaps I'll do that." I realized I still had the locket in my hand and tucked it in the pocket of my dress. So far it had not reacted in any way. As for going to see 'my son', what should I do?

By now, I felt so confused, I doubted my sanity. As for having a son… I had never given birth. I was as certain of that as I could be of anything. But in this situation, where I was living someone else's life, for who knew what purpose, anything might be possible. Perhaps if I saw him and he really was mine, I would feel something. After all, didn't a special bond exist between mother and child? I should feel some stirring of that surely.

From my visits to historic houses, I knew nurseries were invariably tucked away at the top of the house, so I made my way up the next flight of stairs and took care to hold up my skirts so I wouldn't trip.

Through a partially open door, I saw a young woman, dressed differently than the other maids, in a pale blue dress. As she turned and smiled at me, I saw she wore a crisp white apron. She put her finger to her lips. I nodded and tiptoed in. The cot was draped in white lace and I looked down at the sleeping child. He looked so peaceful in his little blue bonnet, with a chubby fist on the pillow. I watched the covers rise and fall with little butterfly movements as he breathed.

I watched and felt...nothing.

It could have been a stranger's baby. It *was* a stranger's baby. I wasn't going mad, just living a nightmare. Alexandra Fletcher still inhabited her own body and, as for Charlotte Devine...well, who knew where she had gone?

The nanny beckoned me outside and closed the door behind her. We moved away into the nursery, where toys lay scattered on the floor.

She tidied them away in a large box as she spoke to me. "Baby's been ever so good, madam. Eating all his food up and playing with his toys. He's a joy to care for, he is. Such a happy wee bairn."

"Good, I'm glad to hear it." I couldn't think of anything else to say. What else should I ask? "And he's been well? No fevers or rashes or anything?"

"Och no, madam. You would be the first to hear if there was anything of concern. No, he's a strong, healthy wee lad."

"That's great," I said. The nanny looked at me, with a bemused frown.

"I mean, thank you. That is most gratifying."

The frown vanished and the smile returned. "As I said, madam, he's a pleasure to look after."

I nodded, smiled and left. Another thought hit me at that moment. Could it be possible that I had literally swapped lives with Charlotte? In 2014, was Greg struggling to cope with an equally confused woman from 1912, who not only missed her husband, however unpleasant he might be, but also grieved for a baby she might never see again?

The thoughts sent shivers up and down my spine.

On the way back down to the room I now knew as the drawing room, my thoughts turned to the voices I had heard. No way had I imagined them. I opened the door and stepped in, but then stopped and clutched my throat.

A woman uncurled herself and slipped from the chaise longue like a serpent leaving its nest, her black hair falling to her waist as she rose, and her long full skirt swaying seductively. But something was wrong with her. Then, as she parted her full lips to speak, I realized I could see straight through her.

Her voice sounded like a distant echo I heard in my head, more than my ears.

"You have come from *her*, haven't you? You have come for my son."

"No, I—I don't know what you mean. Who are you?"

But she didn't need to tell me. I recognized her, shadowy though she might be. And that accent. I'd heard it before. Upstairs in Adrian's room. Then, somehow, I also knew she was the one who had stood behind me and sighed as I examined the locket.

"I am Margarita Garcia Lopez Devine."

I stared at her. She came closer. The now too familiar stench of death came with her and I cowered as I saw, behind the veil of makeup, the pale, shiny bone and hollow eye sockets that reminded me of my specter, who had so far failed to follow me here.

To my horror, she opened her mouth to reveal her bony jaw, drawn back in a rictus grin. Her bare shoulders gleamed as I saw the skeleton beneath and watched the bones work in her shoulder joint as she raised her right arm.

My voice trailed off to a hopeless wail. "Why are you doing this?"

"You do not belong here." Her long, bony arm stretched out in front of her and I backed away, furious with myself for my weakness.

The arm stretched farther and now I forced myself to stand my ground. The sickly, putrefying smell was stronger now. It filled my nostrils. But beneath it lay something much worse. I felt it touch me, looked down and screamed at the wriggling, writhing mass of blackened filth that plopped down onto the carpet between the woman's legs.

Margarita's fingers latched on to my shoulders and squeezed until pain shot through them. The bones weren't clean either. Little bits of rotting flesh hung off them. Her strength overwhelmed me as she pushed me down, until I dropped to my knees.

"No, *please*. No."

Through agonized eyes, I saw her grin widen. The fingers dug in harder, breaking the skin. The revolting mass had crawled back up inside her, but I could see it, curled, fetus-like. Waiting.

The fingers raked my arm, and I dripped blood. Pain enveloped me until I could think of nothing but how to stop it.

Again I screamed. Why didn't the servants come? Surely they could hear me?

Then, in a second, she disappeared. I opened my eyes to an empty room.

My shoulders pulsated with pain and I stared at myself in the mirror. I saw what I expected, my dress torn and bloodied, my shoulder red, and rapidly turning purple. None of that surprised me.

The shock was seeing a blonde girl stare back at me.

Chapter Thirteen

I suppose I lost any sense of being myself during the days that followed. I stared at a stranger in the mirror, washed a stranger in the bath and dressed a stranger every day. Out of my mouth, a stranger spoke and, when Adrian came to me at night, he had sex with a stranger's body. In time, that became my only consolation. As I inhabited another woman's body, I couldn't be unfaithful to my husband. Not that you could call what he did 'making love'. He took what he wanted and left.

I still had my moments, of course, those occasions when I would remember my reason for being there. I would rant and hear a harridan scream out of my mouth. Then Adrian would hold me fast and pour laudanum down my throat and I would drift into merciful oblivion. Each time I woke, I prayed I would find myself back in my own time, but it never happened.

Spring gave way to summer and, on a particularly hot day, Margarita paid me another visit.

I had almost believed I'd invented her presence that day but, one morning, I sat at the dressing table and fingered Grace's locket, failing, yet again, to make a connection with the girl who had owned it.

Charlotte's blue eyes gazed back at me. She was undeniably pretty, in a fragile, doll-like way. Nothing like me physically and, I'm sure, nothing like me mentally either. I was becoming familiar with the contours of her face and the tiny blemishes that kept her milk-white skin from perfection.

A movement on the edge of my vision distracted me and I turned abruptly. Margarita. Cloaked in black lace from head to foot, with a mantilla on her head. Her raven hair was glossy, and she seemed to have more substance than the first time I had seen her. All my senses constricted as she made her slow way forward. Her jet-black eyes fixed on me. I could almost taste her malevolence, like some disgusting cesspit. Again, the smell of putrefied flesh mingled with rotting, rank vegetation and filled the room till I gagged.

She opened her mouth in a wide grimace that showed toothless, rotting gums. All around her, reptilian hissing mingled with the moans and wails of death throes. I clapped my hands over my ears. "Stop. Please stop."

She was almost on top of me now. I screwed my eyes shut. What would she do? Kill me? She pressed herself into me as if trying to absorb me. I opened my eyes and she had changed. Wrapped around me, like some obscene lover, I recognized the hideous mass that had curled inside her. It had fed off her evil and now it was ready for me. I screamed.

It opened its maw. Teeth like steel fangs, a forked tongue, red, elliptical eyes. Scales covered its triangular face. I screamed again. I struggled to free myself but it clung on tighter. It seemed to be trying to enter me, to melt into my skin.

I cried for God to save me, even for death to end this. I screamed for Greg and then, at last, I screamed for Adrian, the only one who might have any chance of ending this.

Abruptly it stopped, as if it had never been there. No smell, no sound. Had I imagined it all? I blinked rapidly as my eyes adjusted to a newly sunny, warm bedroom and I caught my breath. There, at the door, stood Adrian. He was smiling and I saw the welcome bottle in his hand. Laudanum. My new friend. It gave me peace.

"Lie down, my dear. You need to rest."

I obeyed. I had no more fight left in me.

"Adrian, your mother was here. I don't know what she wants from me, but that's why I screamed."

He smiled at me, in a patronizing way he might use to a young child. "There was no one here. You weren't screaming. I merely came to enquire if you would be taking luncheon with me today."

"But—"

"Hush now. Drink this and rest. We will talk later, if you feel well enough."

I sipped the liquid, which tasted less bitter these days. He had taken to adding more brandy to it to make it more palatable. I drank it down gratefully and, just before I closed my eyes, I noticed that, for the first time, he had left the bottle by my bedside.

My opium dreams were peaceful. In them, Greg and I wandered down country lanes, visited places we had never seen together. Rome. Venice. Paris. We sat at the edge of crystal clear lakes and dipped our toes into deliciously inviting water. We laughed, drank wine...and then I woke up to my Edwardian prison.

I never went out. After that first time, Adrian had ordered the servants to keep an eye on me. If I showed any sign of heading for the front door, they barred my way. They seemed to have a sixth sense and magically appeared just in time to suggest a cup of tea or an afternoon nap.

The woman I used to be would have persisted. The woman I had become did as she was told. In the end, I just sipped more laudanum and lay down on the chaise longue.

I don't know how long I could have carried on like that. Drifting in and out of consciousness, going through the motions of eating, bathing, dressing. I existed in a permanent lethargy, where I cared about nothing and barely noted the passage of time.

Adrian received no visitors but, every day, he went out to work. I discovered he owned a brewery, although how he'd acquired it seemed shrouded in some unsavory transaction. Now he seemed happy with my compliant behavior, and he was prepared to part with little snippets of information that some remaining sane morsel of my brain was storing up.

"Mayhew and Sons is doing well now," he told me as he puffed at his after-dinner cigar. "Since I took control away from that fool Josiah Mayhew, profits have increased fourfold."

"Did Mr. Mayhew sell it to you?" I asked as I sipped coffee.

He laughed but there was no mirth in it, just echoes of triumph and disdain. "Sell it? No, Charlotte. Mayhew didn't *sell* it to me, I *took* it from him. I won it in a hand of Baccarat."

Even my befuddled brain railed at this. "He risked everything on the turn of a card?"

"A fool and his money are soon parted. He was forced to sell his mansion and leave Edinburgh in disgrace, so he went down south. Berwick maybe. I heard he shot himself, or drowned, or perhaps both. At any rate, it was no great loss."

"You ruined him."

"I am quite sure he would have done the same to me if I had been as foolish as he was. You are lucky, Charlotte. Your husband knows how to make fortunes, not lose them."

Out of the corner of my eye, I sensed movement in the shadows behind him. For an instant, I was sure I saw his mother's triumphant, smiling face.

"You look as if you've seen a ghost," Adrian said. "Or maybe you're just shocked at how ruthless I can be."

I nodded, not trusting myself to speak, and took another sip of rapidly cooling coffee.

Around me, the air chilled, but Adrian seemed oblivious to it.

He puffed his cigar again and a cloud of purplish smoke drifted upwards.

"I hear you haven't visited our son in weeks. The child will grow up thinking the nanny is his mother."

"And have you? Visited him I mean."

"Yes."

But I doubted it. I resolved to try again, but on the three occasions I had ventured up to the nursery, I had felt nothing. In fact, on the last visit, I had felt a wave of revulsion. Oh, the child was just like any other and the nanny kept him scrupulously clean, but the thought of how he had come to be in this world—that Adrian and the woman I inhabited had made him—sent me off in a choking fit. I had also discovered the child's name. Martyn.

September brought heavy rain and tore the gently turning leaves off the trees, shattering the summer and ushering in an early autumn.

Iris selected warmer dresses for me to wear. I took little interest in what I wore, so I accepted all her suggestions without question. No one but the servants and Adrian would see me anyway, so why bother?

One streaming wet morning, I was, as usual, lying on the chaise longue. I'd just drunk my morning coffee and was about to reach for my laudanum when I heard a commotion in the hall. I tidied my dress and went to investigate.

Adrian was out at work and to my amazement, I saw Sarah and the butler— Steddings—manhandling a distraught woman out of the door.

"What's going on?" I said.

Steddings had his arm up the struggling woman's back. "This woman asked to see the master, madam. Sarah explained that he will not be returning until this evening, but she refuses to leave."

"I'll see her." I surprised myself by the force of my words. The woman stopped struggling.

Steddings and Sarah exchanged questioning glances, but the butler relaxed his grip.

I stood aside and indicated the open door. "Please, come in and tell me how I can help you."

The woman shrugged off Steddings, and moved towards me, a grateful look on her face.

"Please bring fresh coffee," I said to Sarah and then closed the door. "I'm Al…" I hesitated, but there really was nothing for it in the circumstances. "Mrs. Devine. I'm afraid my…husband is out at work now, but if I can help, I'll be happy to do so, but I'm afraid I don't know your name."

"Louisa. Louisa Mayhew." She burst into tears and her hands shook so violently she could barely unclasp her bag. I helped her and she took out a lace trimmed handkerchief. As she dried her eyes, her voice shook. "I'm sorry, Mrs. Devine. I was so determined to hold back my grief today, but I…"

She burst into tears again and, on impulse, I put my arms around her to comfort her. Finally, her sobbing subsided and she seemed ready to speak. I moved away and sat on a chair opposite. Coffee arrived and

Sarah seemed in no hurry to leave. Had she been told by Steddings to hang around and report back what she overheard?

"Thank you, Sarah," I said. "I can take it from here."

She hesitated, then bobbed her usual curtsey and left. I followed her to make sure she carried on to the door leading to the servants' hall. Satisfied, I closed the drawing room door firmly and returned to Mrs. Mayhew.

I poured her a coffee and handed it to her.

"What must you think of me? Invading your house, demanding to speak to your husband and then making such a scene. I must apologize for my actions."

"No, Mrs. Mayhew, there's no need to apologize. I've a feeling I know why you're here."

She lowered her eyes and I was afraid the floodgates were about to reopen but, this time, she contained herself.

"I don't know how much you know about your husband's business dealings."

"If your husband was Josiah Mayhew, I believe I know a little and, if what I've heard is true, I want you to know that I believe Adrian Devine's actions to be beyond contempt."

She looked as if I had just proved the earth was flat after all.

"My husband was indeed Josiah Mayhew. Your husband stole his brewery from him, cheating at cards—"

"*Cheating?* He told me he'd won it in a game of Baccarat and that's bad enough, but... Are you sure Adrian cheated?"

Mrs. Mayhew nodded. "I have it on the best authority possible. A former friend of your husband's, who had little time for Josiah, saw the whole thing and came to me. That is why I'm here. I've come to try and persuade your husband to grant us some money from the profits. I understand the brewery is doing exceedingly well and I thought, maybe, in the circumstances, he could be convinced to help us..." Her voice faltered and only then did I notice the shabbiness of her once fine coat. The cuffs were frayed and the elbows were worn and shiny. Her boots were down at heel and scuffed.

"We have nothing, Mrs. Devine. Nothing. My children and I have gone from living in a beautiful home, not a mile from here, to one room in Berwick, and now it's even worse. Yesterday, we were evicted because we can't pay the rent. I cannot find work. I can do nothing. I have no skills at all. Except…"

I knew what she meant. In her situation in those days, women ended up on the streets and, at her age—I gauged around forty—hers would be a niche market at best.

"How old are your children?" I asked.

"George is eleven and Eleanor is thirteen. Only the good Lord Himself knows what will become of them." Fresh tears streamed down her face.

I listened as Louisa Mayhew told me about her husband's first meeting with Adrian. I noticed that, every so often, a cloud seemed to pass over her face. At first, I put it down to the miserable memories she was recounting, but I began to have doubts as, each time, her gaze switched from me to somewhere over my left shoulder.

She told me that Josiah Mayhew had first met Adrian in a prestigious Edinburgh hotel where they were both guests of an American financier. Adrian had engaged Josiah in conversation before inviting him to play Baccarat with some other acquaintances of his, including, it appeared, the current whistleblower who had been responsible for Louisa's visit today.

"My husband wasn't the strongest of men, Mrs. Devine. He could be easily persuaded down the wrong path. Your husband has a silver tongue. Apparently he's noted for it, along with his utter ruthlessness. His acquaintance said he will stop at nothing to get what he wants and that's exactly what he did. I had no idea what was going on. Josiah went out frequently in the evenings, meeting with other brewers, and potential buyers. He liked to be at the center of it all, you see. I used to tell him to let his employees do it, but he said, where's the fun in that?"

She needed another pause, to dry her eyes. I said nothing, letting the picture of Adrian Devine develop in my mind. I knew he was callous and capable of murder and nothing this woman said overly surprised me, but she hadn't finished yet.

"I learned later that, over the next six months, your husband played Baccarat with Josiah on at least a dozen occasions. Each time, he raised the stake and he boasted that he would take my husband for every penny. People begged him to stop, but he said he wouldn't until he had everything that had been Josiah's. All his money and property. He said he would laugh as we were run out of town. He'd found an ingenious way to cheat, you see. Only the gentleman who told me knew how he did it. But, with that ability, your husband had already made a fortune out of gambling. Now he has made his second fortune, by rendering us penniless. He stole Mayhew and Sons nine months ago. Last month, my husband got up in the middle of the night, went down to the lakeside and shot himself. He must have fallen in the water, because they took his body out the next day."

She wept silently and I searched for some words of comfort, but couldn't find any. Oh yes, I could promise to talk to Adrian—to confront him even—but would he listen or do anything to make amends? Not the Adrian I had seen.

I looked around. If I could see some valuable object that she could sell, perhaps that would help.

"Where are you staying? Are you back in Edinburgh now?"

She nodded, her eyes red and watery. "I have an aunt who has kindly allowed us to stay in one room until her son returns from India. She's my only living relative and has precious little money of her own, so we cannot stay there for more than a few weeks at best."

I stood and moved around the room, picking up objects and examining them for hallmarks.

"What are you doing?" she asked.

"Trying to find something I can give you to sell. Until I can think of a better, more permanent solution, I could perhaps let you have items that could bring in a bit of money."

She smiled. "That is so kind of you, but I don't want to put you in any danger. I am told he has an evil temper. I came here with the intention of shaming him into doing the right thing."

"Sadly, I don't think he understands the concept of shame."

Again I noticed her looking over my shoulder. I had to ask. "What do you keep looking at?"

She shook her head and lowered her eyes. "It's the young girl. She's standing behind you and has her hand on your arm. She keeps smiling at me and touching a locket around her neck."

"Young girl?" I spun around.

"She's gone now."

"Can you describe her to me?"

"Slim, quite tall, around fourteen or fifteen. She's wearing a white dress with little flowers on it and carrying a fur trimmed hat. The locket is oval…"

"Like this one?"

I handed her Grace's silver locket I had taken to carrying in my pocket every day.

"The very same."

"Take it." I thrust it at her. For some reason, I knew this was what Grace wanted, a chance to help someone else who had been wronged by her stepbrother. He'd had no business taking it anyway.

"I couldn't possibly."

"No, please. It belonged to her. She wants you to have it. I believe my husband stole it from someone else he wronged—its rightful owner." It all made sense. When they found Grace's body, her locket had been tangled in her fingers as I had seen it on the painting. No doubt it would have been given to Jonas and Adrian took it, probably to spite the father who had thrown him out.

The woman put out a tentative hand and took the locket from me.

"It's heavier than it looks," she said, turning it over in her hand.

"You may wish to throw the photograph away. It's of Adrian."

"Don't you want it?"

I shook my head. "No more than I want him. The locket's pure silver. It should fetch you a little and take this as well." I handed her a heavy, solid silver cigarette box. Adrian would miss that before the locket, but I didn't care. What was the loss of a cigarette box compared to what this poor woman had endured at his hands? I wouldn't let the servants take the blame. When he noticed it missing, I'd confess what I'd done and why. He could do what he liked. I no longer cared and, surprisingly, realized I was no longer scared of him.

She eyed me curiously but I didn't feel inclined to elaborate. "Have you seen many ghosts, Mrs. Mayhew?"

She opened her mouth to speak, then closed it again. I nodded at her to try and encourage her to say whatever was on her mind.

She sighed and shook her head. "If I tell you I do, then you will think me insane."

"I can assure you I won't. You've just described a young girl I've seen myself. If you're mad, then so am I. And believe me, Mrs. Mayhew, despite my bizarre situation, I'm perfectly sane."

Mrs. Mayhew seemed a little taken aback. "Bizarre? I'm sorry, I don't understand."

It would have been a huge relief to unburden myself and share my strange experiences, but I hardly knew this woman and, besides, she already had enough problems of her own.

"Another time, perhaps." I smiled at the irony of my words. Another time in all senses of the term.

Mrs. Mayhew moistened her lips. "I do see things sometimes—out of the corner of my eye mainly—but it's unusual for me to have such a clear vision as I had of that girl. I sense things too. Things that aren't quite right. Things that seem...out of place, somehow. Like you."

This was unexpected. "What do you see when you look at me?" I asked.

"An attractive young woman who doesn't belong here." Her eyes opened wider. "I'm so sorry, Mrs. Devine, I had no wish to offend you. You've been so kind."

"No offense taken. Please continue."

"That's it really. I see an attractive, dark-haired, young—"

"*Dark*-haired? You see me with dark hair?"

"Doesn't everyone? You have dark brown hair."

"And my eyes?"

"Brown. I'm sorry, I'm really confused now. Why wouldn't I see you with dark brown hair?"

I took a deep breath. "Because everyone else here sees me as a blonde."

"Pardon?"

I reached for the album Adrian had shown me and flicked through the leaves until I came to the photograph of Adrian and his wife on their wedding day.

Mrs. Mayhew drew closer and I pointed at Charlotte.

"Is that who you see when you look at me?"

Mrs. Mayhew stared at it as if beginning to doubt my sanity.

"No, not at all. You look nothing like her."

"Her name is Charlotte Devine and she is married to Adrian. Until recently, I had to look at my reflected image through a second mirror to see her, but now it's her I see all the time." I felt tears well up.

Mrs. Mayhew looked from me to the photograph and back again. Panic registered on her face. "I'm sorry, Mrs. Devine, I don't understand any of this, I'm afraid. I'll have to go. Thank you so much for your help."

I could do nothing but watch as she stuffed the locket and cigarette box in her bag and scurried to the door.

"Mrs. Mayhew, please let me know where I can contact you so that—" The slamming of the front door behind her cut me off.

Weeks of pent-up fury, grief and emotion piled on top of me and I burst into tears. I was still crying half an hour later when Adrian came back.

At the sight of me, he scowled. "What have you got to cry about?"

Through my tears, I said, "You would too if you'd lost everything that ever meant anything to you."

"Don't be ridiculous! Everything you need is here. Make the best of it."

I grasped the chair arm until my knuckles turned white. Not this time. Pussyfooting around him had achieved nothing. I wouldn't hold back any longer. I would find out what he knew.

"How *dare* you pretend you know nothing of what's happened here. Six months ago, I was on holiday with my husband—my real husband—in Edinburgh, in 2014. I was looking for Adrian Devine's nearest surviving relative and that brought me to your son, Martyn. Then you came into the room, looking precisely as you do now. At first, I didn't believe it possible, but now I know it's true. Somehow or other, you have discovered the secret of immortality, and a youthful one at that. So Grace's curse has had no adverse effect whatsoever. You have everything you want. Money, power, success. Surely it wouldn't do you any harm to forgive Grace for cursing you. That's all she needs to stop her from her endlessly wandering, hovering between this world and the next. And, after what you did to her, it's the least you can do."

We stood in stony silence for a few seconds until Adrian began a slow handclap.

"Oh, very good, Charlotte. Very erudite. Insane, of course. You are completely mad. I should have you locked up in an asylum."

"Come on, Adrian. You and I both know I'm not insane. For reasons I can't possibly imagine, you've brought me back here, maybe because this is the time in which you really belong. By rights you should have been dead decades before 2014. So how did you do it? And where's your real wife? With my husband? Lost in time just as I am and longing to come home? Why have you done this, Adrian? *Why?*"

I saw his olive-skinned face blanch and his eyes grow rounder. He opened his mouth and pointed behind me.

I braced myself and turned around.

Grace stood at the back of the room. One hand clutched the silk ribbons of her hat and I noticed she no longer wore the locket. Her expression was blank as she stared, not at me, but at Adrian. Her mouth moved and I would swear she mouthed, "Forgive me."

Adrian whimpered behind me. Then I heard him rush to the door. It slammed behind him and Grace faded from view.

I sank into the nearest chair, my head in my hands. What was I supposed to do now? Was I wrong about Adrian? Did the man in 1912 not know what was to come? Had other forces been at work, sending me back here? Whatever the answer, all the signs pointed to Grace, especially as she had just manifested herself, not just to me, but to the person whose forgiveness she craved.

Chapter Fourteen

"Where's the cigarette box?" Adrian had clearly put aside yesterday's unnerving experience. His usual arrogant self had returned.

"If you mean the large, silver one in the drawing room, I gave it to a deserving cause."

He advanced towards me, his right hand balled into a fist, but he stopped short, just inches away. I forced myself to stand my ground.

"What deserving cause?" he said.

I took a deep breath. "Mrs. Mayhew. She and her children are homeless and starving, thanks to you."

Now both hands were tightly clenched and I prepared to duck.

"You *bitch!* How *dare* you consort with my enemies!"

"Your enemies? Whatever has that poor woman ever done to you?"

"She was fool enough to marry that idiot, Mayhew, and stupid enough to bear his children. She deserves everything she gets. And *nothing*, do you hear me? *Nothing* from me. I presume she came here, begging for scraps? I shall instruct Steddings that she is not to be allowed in this house. That cigarette box was Regency and very valuable."

"Good. Perhaps it'll keep her children fed and clothed for a while."

This time, I didn't see the punch coming. I staggered backwards and fell onto the chaise longue, gasping and clutching at my injured chest, but he wasn't finished with me yet.

"Don't you *ever* do that again," he said, "or there'll be plenty more where that came from, I assure you."

Tears sprang to my eyes, adding to my anger. "You *bastard!*"

My voice must have been heard outside that room but no one came to investigate. Not then, nor when my cries of anger turned to screams of pain. Adrian rained down blows on my head. He threw me off the chaise longue onto the floor and kicked and punched me in the stomach as I struggled, desperate to curl into a fetal position and protect myself from the worst of his violence.

I thought he wouldn't let up until he'd killed me, but, after delivering one last vicious kick in my kidneys, he stopped. Tears streamed down my face. Knives of pain stabbed at me from almost every part of my body. Whether by accident or design, he had, at least, left my face alone, but my head throbbed from where he repeatedly banged it against the floor.

"Let that be a lesson you don't forget in a hurry."

He left me huddled on the carpet.

I lay there, the pain too raw for me to move. In 2014, I could have had him arrested for aggravated assault, maybe even attempted murder, and he would have been locked up. But in 1912, I was a married woman, largely unprotected by the law. He was, allegedly, my husband and had the right to discipline his wife pretty much as he so wished.

I had to find a way to end this. After a few minutes, I gritted my teeth and gripped the chaise longue. I dragged myself to my feet. Every breath strained my muscles and sent new shards of pain through my ribs as they pressed painfully against the corset stays. That would surely have to go now. As soon as I could struggle upstairs, I would remove the hateful thing once and for all.

I let go of the chaise longue and prayed I wouldn't topple over. The bell pull was still six feet away and I shuffled towards it. Iris could help me up the stairs and off with my clothes. Let her see the results of her mistress's vicious beating at the hands of her thug of a husband. At least I'd have a witness if I could ever put him behind bars.

She did her best to conceal her shock, as bruise after bruise, wheal after wheal was revealed. My maid said nothing, but I heard a sharp intake of breath on more than one occasion. Reflected in the mirror, I could see he had done a pretty thorough job on my chest, ribs and arms. When I turned and looked over my shoulder, deep red marks covered my back, where he had kicked me.

Every garment removed came at the price of fresh torment but, finally, I was dressed only in my loose nightgown.

I just wanted to sleep and was grateful for the little bottle of laudanum, steeped in brandy, that sat on the night table, along with its little crystal tumbler.

Iris pulled back the covers and I crawled into bed. I reached for the laudanum and my hand shook, but my maid rescued the glass from me and poured out a dose. I nodded my thanks and then regretted it as the sudden movement jarred my pounding head.

I drank the mixture straight down and handed the glass back to Iris. She spoke for the first time since I had summoned her. "Is there anything else you require, madam? Some soup perhaps, or a nice hot cup of tea?"

I smiled at her. She felt sorry for me and wanted to help, but I just wanted the laudanum to kick in, so I could drift away from my pain.

"Thank you, Iris, but I'd like to sleep now."

She hesitated, then nodded, curtsied and slipped out of the room, closing the door quietly behind her. No doubt, yet again, the servants would have a lot to gossip about over their dinner.

The next day, Adrian behaved as if nothing had happened. I was determined to come down for breakfast, as a gesture of defiance more than any need to eat. I wore a loose fitting gown, but he made no comment on my appearance or on my hair. My head felt too sore for clips and even gentle brushing hurt like hell.

Today, I would find some way of forcing him into forgiving Grace. I had the merest germ of an idea, flimsy at best, but all I could come up with. Adrian had been frightened of Grace when she had appeared. What if I could get her to return? What if she could frighten him into forgiving her? It was worth a try at least. What did I have to lose?

I took a sip of tea and Louisa Mayhew's strained and anxious face sprang into my mind. If only I could help her too. Hopefully she would get a good price for that cigarette box and locket, but that wouldn't last forever. If I could just get Adrian so scared that he agreed to sign over a regular income or lump sum to her as well, then some measure of justice would be done. Then, please God, somehow I could return to my own time.

I couldn't allow myself to think I'd be trapped here forever. That thought brought me nothing but grief —not to mention my growing addiction to laudanum. Well, if I carried that with me to 2014, I would just have to check into rehab. At least in my time they had more civilized methods of coping with addiction. Here, they'd probably sling me into Bedlam and throw away the key.

Steddings disturbed me one morning, a week after my beating. I could move a little easier, although the bruising still hadn't fully come out. As he opened the door, I was startled to see he held his silver letter tray in his gloved hand. He offered it to me.

"A young boy delivered this for you, madam. He was most particular that I hand it to you personally."

I stared at the small white envelope. It seemed good quality and the handwriting was very neat. Grandma used to talk about the days when people prided themselves on having a 'good hand'. Strange I was thinking about her more and more with each passing day. Maybe because of my circumstances. She had only been a child in 1912. Mary Eleanor Croft, born January 24th 1902. She had been forty when my mother was born. Strange that Grace had been my mother's middle name. Grandma had insisted on it. Something about that niggled me, but right then I had this letter to deal with.

'Mrs. A. Devine'.

Charlotte hadn't received one letter since I had been there, although, as all the mail was handed to Adrian, he might have been withholding them.

I picked up the envelope, but didn't want Steddings around when I opened it, sure he would scrutinize me for any reaction. I doubted I could trust him but, by letting me have this letter, he had probably already overstepped the mark. If he told his master, and couldn't add any more information, he would be in danger of incurring Adrian's anger. As things stood, Steddings and I both had good reason to keep quiet about the letter's existence.

"Thank you, Steddings. That will be all."

His expression never wavered. Now I know the true meaning of inscrutable.

With the butler gone, I ripped open the envelope with shaking fingers, unfolded the small sheet of paper and looked for the signature. "Louisa Mayhew". My eyes swept back to the top of the letter.

> *Dear Mrs. Devine,*
>
> *Please forgive me for my undignified and hasty departure last week and accept my sincere, heartfelt thanks for the property you gave me, which I have since been able to sell for a tidy sum. It has meant that I have found small, but respectable, lodgings for myself and my children. Yesterday, I secured a position in the ladies' department at Jenner's store on Princes Street. It seems my earlier life has equipped me to be able to advise ladies of quality! I am to commence on Monday.*
>
> *Today, quite by chance, I came across a former friend of my late husband, who knows Mr. Devine very well. He told me something which means I must see you urgently, for it concerns your situation. I believe you are in the gravest of all possible dangers, for I now know things about Mr. Devine I would never have thought to hear about any human being. I trust my husband's friend implicitly, for he is the most upright and sober of gentlemen.*
>
> *Please meet me at the Highland Rose Café, on the corner of Bracken Street and De Villiers Road at three tomorrow afternoon. I will wait a further hour in case*

*you are delayed, but I must stress the urgency of our
meeting. I really am most concerned for your safety.*

    I remain, yours sincerely

    Louisa Mayhew

I folded the note as a familiar prickling of fear started up in my stomach. Somehow I must get out of here and meet her, but how would I do that?

Since my barbarous beating, Iris had opened up and become much more attentive and sympathetic. Could I enlist her help? There were risks, but if I didn't take them, I would be stuck here for sure.

The risks for Iris would be considerable too. If she was caught helping me escape, she would be out of a job, on the streets without a reference. A gentle girl like that would find it hard to survive.

But however hard I tried, I could see no alternative but to ask her to help me. With no access to any keys in this place, I couldn't even unlock a door. Adrian said my incarceration was for the good of my health, that I was clearly in a fragile mental state, the streets were harsh and the air rank. He didn't want me to deteriorate. Always that veiled threat of the asylum hung in the air, to keep me acquiescent, and reaching for the laudanum. Well, that would have to stop, right now! I had to break this downward spiral. Whatever Louisa Mayhew had discovered, it concerned me and might even provide the answers I couldn't find myself.

A fire burned in the grate. I tore the letter into tiny scraps and watched them burn to ashes. Adrian would never know.

I rang for Iris. Sarah responded and hurried away to fetch her.

My maid fiddled with a lock of hair that had escaped from her cap.

"Are you all right, Iris? You look a little flushed."

A wobbly smile forced its way onto her lips. "Thank you, madam, for your concern, but I'm quite well, thank you. Is there something I can get for you?"

The words were formal but at least her tone was warm.

"Yes, there is, but it's vital you tell no one what I am about to ask you to do. Is that clear?"

Iris's eyes had grown wider and now she was staring at me, blinking. I could hardly hear her hushed whisper. "Yes, madam."

"Good. I need to meet a friend tomorrow afternoon and I need your help to get out of here and then return some time later. I'm not sure how long I'll be, but I need someone with access to the keys. Could you do that for me? Would you?"

She stared at me as if I had just asked her to leap off a mountain. "Oh, madam, I…"

I took her hands in mine. I could tell her mind was in turmoil and prayed she would agree. After all, I could hardly force her to go against Adrian's express orders, which, no doubt, had been reinforced regularly by Steddings.

As I was about to give up hope, she nodded. "Yes, madam, I will help you. I didn't say anything, because it's not my place, but I thought it was terrible what the master did to you last week. Awful."

I squeezed her hands and released them. "I can't thank you enough. Now I need to be at the Highland Rose Café by three o'clock. Do you know where that is?"

Iris nodded. "I think it's best you don't leave by the front door, or by the servants' entrance. There's too much chance of you being seen. You're better off using the French windows."

I followed her gaze over to the tall glass doors, kept permanently locked, like everything else in this fortress.

"You have the key?"

"I know where it is. Mr. Steddings keeps it on a hook in his parlor. He'll be having his afternoon nap then, so I can get it, unlock the door, replace the key and then, when you return, you ring for me and I can bring the key back to lock up." Her face clouded over. "Do you have any idea when that will be? Only Mr. Steddings is usually around again at a little after four and the master gets back any time after five, as you know."

"I'll be as quick as possible, I promise."

"Very well, madam. It's very easy to find and I'll tell you where to get a cab. If you ring for me at half past two, I'll come up and let you out."

"Iris, I don't know how to thank you."

"I'm happy to help you, madam. I just hope your friend can also help you find how to return to your real life."

"Real life? What do you mean, Iris?"

She shifted uncomfortably. "I'm not supposed to say anything. I'm not really supposed to know. But a few months ago, Mr. Steddings told us that he had caught the master consorting with the 'dark forces', as he put it. We all thought he had been at the sherry or maybe the master's brandy, but he hadn't. He was stone cold sober. And then, all of a sudden, one afternoon, you were...different. You spoke differently. Oh your voice was the same, but the words you used. They weren't what we're used to. You still looked the same—"

"Not to everyone, it would seem."

Iris's eyes held questions, but I didn't have time to answer them and involve the girl in an even more incredible story than the one she was telling me.

"Then there's the things you do differently. We're not supposed to notice, but Cook complained to Mr. Steddings that you seemed to have forgotten how to run the household. She had to guide you through the menus for the week and remind you about the household accounts."

She was right. I hadn't a clue how to run a household, even a small one like this where the staff was perfectly capable of doing it all unaided. I just let the cook get on with it and Steddings direct operations. I had no idea I had caused such consternation below stairs.

"Then there's young master Martyn. You would always see him at teatime, every day, without fail, but you suddenly stopped and now you hardly ever go up to the nursery. Nanny says she's not sure you even know her name anymore. You just stay in this room, day after day, until it's time to go to bed." She clapped her hand over her mouth. "Oh, I'm sorry, madam. I'm speaking out of turn. It's not my place to question you, or anything you do."

"Not at all. I wish we'd had this conversation weeks ago."

"Begging your pardon, madam, but that's a bit difficult, because usually by this time you're fast asleep on the chaise longue."

She was right, of course. Bored witless by my existence, frustrated by my inability to do what needed to be done, the laudanum called straight after lunch and that was it, until the time came to change for dinner.

"Was it very different before? I mean, before I came on the scene."

Iris frowned. "'On the scene'? That's another expression I've never heard before."

"I mean, when the old Mrs. Devine was here; the one you remember."

"Oh, yes, I see. Well Mr. and Mrs. Devine led a very quiet life for such young people. Mrs. Devine stayed at home most days, only occasionally receiving visitors. She used to potter about in her garden and read. Well, then Mr. Devine said that you'd had a funny turn and needed to be kept totally quiet. That's why the house and all the windows had to be locked, to keep you from escaping and doing harm to yourself. The others still believe that's true, but they don't know you like I do. And they haven't seen the bruises."

"Did Mr. Devine ever hit his wife before?"

Iris shook her head. "I've heard him speak sharply to her, but she never argued with him like you do. That seems to get him all riled up."

"Where I come from, what he did would put him in prison for a very long time."

"Where *do* you come from?"

Should I? "Maybe one day, I'll tell you, but not now. We have a lot to do. Please start by getting rid of the contents of every bottle of laudanum in this house."

Her eyes widened again. "But what if the master finds out?"

"What's he going to do? Drink the stuff? Don't worry, Iris, just dilute some brandy a little and pour it into the bottles. He'll never know the difference."

Iris took the bottle and left me alone to my thoughts.

I wasn't alone long.

It started as a slight darkening of a shadow in the corner of the room. Then came the whispers, vague and indistinct. I couldn't make out any words until the shape shot across the room and a voice echoed in my ear.

"You shall not destroy my son. He is mine. You shall not have him."

A furious hissing threatened to deafen me. I clapped my hands over my ears. "I don't want him. I want him to release his stepsister."

"You *lie*. You have come from *her*. She wants to take him away from me."

The shape swirled around the room like smoke vapor and again that rank stench of death and decay filled my senses.

I retched. "I don't know what you want from me. I don't know what you're talking about. I'm trying to help Grace."

"You *lie*."

I sank to my knees on the floor and covered my head with my hands, terrified of what was to come. The awful vapor surrounded me, choking me. I couldn't breathe.

"You *lie*," it said again, the terrible hissing stronger than ever.

Something struck me and I toppled over. Then it was gone. But it had left something behind. A terrible feeling of despair that stuck firm in my stomach and refused to go away.

Chapter Fifteen

I arrived, out of breath, at the Highland Rose Café, just ten minutes late. So far, everything had worked perfectly. Iris had answered my call and let me out of the French windows. Earlier, she'd managed to sneak Charlotte's coat, hat, gloves and boots into the drawing room, where she had hidden them in a variety of places. I admired her ingenuity, although my coat was a little creased from being placed under the cushions of the Chesterfield.

Once out of the garden gate, I melted into the throng of the other smart Edwardians. I took care to keep my head demurely lowered and walked with little, ladylike steps. I wanted to do nothing to draw attention to myself and hoped and prayed Adrian wouldn't break with his normal habits and decide to wander around Edinburgh's fashionable streets, or come home early.

I hailed a cab at the end of the road. My maid had somehow managed to scrape up the return fare and I had to return it to her as soon as possible.

The journey had taken a little longer than she had suggested, but now, here I was, feeling surreal and with a frisson of fear running up my spine. What was so important Louisa had to see me so urgently?

I opened the glass paneled door and entered the warm café. Smells of fresh coffee mingled with equally fresh baking. In display cases, delicious-looking cakes and buns competed for attention. I looked around the room and then I saw her. Louisa Mayhew gave a slight wave and I wove my way past crowded tables to get to her. She had chosen well; this was a perfect place to get lost in. The thrum of conversation was loud enough to drown out any individual words. No one would pay us any attention and we could be anonymous here.

"I'm so glad you came, Mrs. Devine."

"Oh, please, call me Alex." I couldn't bring myself to use Charlotte's name.

Louisa looked perplexed for a moment, but my smile must have reassured her. She nodded. I sat down, placed Charlotte's handbag on the floor beside me and peeled off my gloves.

"I've ordered tea for two. I hope that's acceptable?"

"Thank you, Louisa. That's great."

Again, she gave me a little smile. No doubt my odd turn of phrase had amused her too.

Louisa poured out a cup of tea for me and took a sip of her own. I didn't have to wait long for her to begin.

"May I first say that I still don't understand much of what you told me when we last met, but I think that you will not think me foolish or mad when I tell you what I have learned from my late husband's friend. I can only hope you will take it seriously and take appropriate action before it is too late." She paused and studied me.

"Please go on, Louisa."

"Very well. It seems that one day, about a year ago, Henry—that's my husband's friend—was with Mr. Devine at some function where your husband drank rather more brandy than was good for him. Henry said he seemed troubled, as if he had something momentous on his mind. Eventually, there were just the two of them and he clearly wanted to unburden himself. Henry was anxious to get away but, as Mr. Devine began to speak, he became increasingly fascinated and horrified by what he heard. I will warn you, Alex, it's a bizarre story. Henry said he thinks Mr. Devine is—well—not quite right." She tapped her forehead and took another sip of tea.

I wanted to tell her to hurry up and get to the point. Time was passing all too quickly, but I knew I would just have to be patient.

She replaced her cup carefully in its saucer and took a deep breath. "Mr. Devine told Henry that his father had thrown him out of the family home nine years previously. He turned him out without a penny, or at least not enough for a man of his character to last more than a few months, at best. With nowhere to go, Mr. Devine made his way to Edinburgh, where he hoped family would accommodate him, but he found all doors shut to him. He tried to find work, but no one would hire him and, as everything he touched failed, he began to believe he had been cursed.

"Then, one night, as he lay shivering in a cheap boarding house, with nothing but a few pennies to his name, he saw a vision of his late mother. She told him he had indeed been cursed, by his late stepsister, and that she craved forgiveness for her heinous act. But his mother told him not to do it. She told him the girl deserved to suffer. His father should never have remarried and Grace had no right to usurp his father's love. His mother said, if Mr. Devine promised not to forgive his stepsister, she would help him achieve wealth and position. So, he entered into a pact with her."

As I listened to her, the jigsaw began to fall into place. A mother, whose possessive love for her son was so strong, it reached out beyond the grave, determined to destroy anyone she perceived as a threat. Right now, given my bond with Grace, I posed just such a threat.

Louisa placed her gloved hand over mine. "Alex, when I was in your drawing room, I sensed a presence. Not just the young girl. Someone else." She withdrew her hand and shivered. "Something of pure evil is in that house."

"I know. I've seen her. Whatever Adrian's mother has become attacked me yesterday." I told her about the encounter. "She accused me of lying when I said all I wanted was forgiveness for Grace. She said Grace wanted to steal Adrian from her."

"Mr. Devine told Henry that he was paying a heavy price for his mother's help," Louisa said. "His soul is forfeit to her, but he believes that someone will come, to intercede for his stepsister, and it is my belief that person is you. He told Henry that, when that day comes, he must bring you back here, to this time and place, and incarcerate you in an asylum for the rest of your days. Only in that way will he be free of Grace's vengeful spirit."

Incredulous, I stared at her. "But Grace doesn't have a vengeful spirit. All she wants is to be forgiven for uttering the damn curse in the first place. Then she can pass over and rest in peace. Until that happens, she'll just remain earthbound."

Louisa shrugged. "Henry was adamant that this is what Mr. Devine believes. He also believes he has the power to move freely from the present to the future and back again, at will. He told Henry he has lived to see two world wars, a man on the moon, something called a computer, and many strange and wonderful things. Does any of that make any sense to you?"

Despite my growing anxiety, I smiled. "Oh, yes, Louisa. In my time, we take computers for granted. Almost all of us carry small telephones in our pockets and we can communicate with the world on little machines."

"My goodness! So it's true then!" Her face clouded over. "But if that's the case, you really are in danger. He must mean to drive you mad."

"There have been times when I thought he'd already done that. I actually began to believe I could be Charlotte Devine and maybe I'd lost my memory. Now, I believe it was all the laudanum I was taking, but there have been days when I almost gave up."

"You mustn't do that, Alex. Promise me you won't."

I squeezed her hand. "I won't, any more than you will." She smiled.

I felt a chilly blast as the door opened. I had my back to it and couldn't see what Louisa saw, but her horrified look confirmed my worst fears.

"Charlotte."

I gripped the table and turned my head.

Adrian's face was almost purple with rage. "You are coming with me now."

A few heads turned in our direction.

He kept his voice low. "You will come with me now, and you will say nothing, or I shall have this woman arrested for the common thief she is."

"Alex…" Louisa's voice was little more than a whimper.

"Don't worry, I won't cause a scene," I said to her and pushed my chair back, glad it caught Adrian in the thighs, so he had to step back.

He gripped my arm more firmly than necessary but I refused to wince. Tomorrow I would have yet more bruises.

A cab was waiting and Adrian virtually threw me into it. "I will deal with you at home," he said in a furious whisper.

All through the short journey, I tried to think how I could escape that hateful house. And how would I face Iris? Could I ever repay her for her kindness? Then, dominating all my considerations, Grace. I had come so far, endured so much, I couldn't fail her now.

Adrian half-dragged me out of the cab and propelled me up the drive.

Steddings anticipated our arrival and held the door open. I caught his eye— expressionless as ever.

Adrian dragged me into the drawing room and slammed the door. "What the hell did you think you were doing?"

"You can't keep me locked up here forever, Adrian. I had to find out the truth. What *did* your mother tell you on her deathbed? Half an hour she spent, whispering in your ear. What did she pass on to you?"

Adrian said nothing, but, for a moment, his confidence seemed to waver. "How did you know about that?"

"Someone in Arnsay told me. A relative of yours. Did your mother pass on her evil to you? Come on, Adrian, what did she say?"

For once, he seemed to have let his guard down. "My mother had the gift. She could see into the future and she knew father would marry again. She told me the new wife would have a child who would usurp my father's love. I must rid myself of her and secure my inheritance."

"So you let Grace drown. But it backfired, didn't it? Your father disowned you."

His face grew angry again and I could see a vein throb at his temple. "She robbed me of my inheritance and destroyed everything I touched. But there was a way, and Mama found it. She overturned the curse and I became what she had always intended me to be. Rich, powerful. And then you came along. Without you, Grace could never have found me. Now she has. I should kill you right now with my bare hands."

I backed away, but the moment passed and I took my chance. "Grace doesn't want to destroy you, Adrian. She merely wants your forgiveness, so she can pass over and rest in peace."

To my astonishment, Adrian started to laugh. He poured himself a brandy. "Is that what you believe? She would take everything my mother has helped me achieve and destroy it. But she can't do anything without you. She feeds off you like a parasite, but if I killed you, her spirit would be released into the world. At least while she remains tied to you, she can die with you—in time."

"In the asylum you mean?"

This time, he didn't respond, but I knew that was precisely what he intended. I had to try and make him understand. "Adrian, can't you see? The Grace you describe never existed. Your mother created these myths to keep you under her control. Her powers are pure evil and you've paid for her help with your soul. You belong to *her* now. Grace had nothing to do with it."

Adrian threw the glass across the room. It smashed against the wall.

At least he used his open hand, and not his fist, when he slapped me across the face. My teeth cut into my cheek and I tasted blood, but it only served to quicken the adrenalin flow. I had to act now, while I still could, because I wasn't the only one in danger. "What have you done with Iris?"

As if nothing untoward had happened, he poured himself another brandy. "That is none of your concern."

Something in his eyes struck fear into me. "Where is she? What have you done with her?"

"She is where a sniveling little traitor belongs. Steddings caught the stupid girl returning the key to the French windows."

"How did you find me?"

His laugh was hollow. "Iris was persuaded to part with the information."

Surely he wouldn't torture her? But one look at him and I was prepared to believe it.

"I demand to know where she is and what you've done to her."

"Demand? Oh, I don't think you're in any position to make demands."

"Is she still in this house?"

"Yes."

"Then I want to see her. Now. She's my lady's maid and I *need* to see her."

"She *was* your lady's maid. Sarah will assume that role for the time being."

"Sarah's not a lady's maid. She's a parlor maid."

"Sarah is whatever I say she is."

"Then you run a very strange house, Adrian. Anything to do with the servants is my business since you choose to insist I am your wife."

I thought he was going to strike me again, but he didn't. Instead, his face turned white and he backed away.

"She's here again, isn't she? You can see her. Grace."

I don't even know if he heard me. His eyes were transfixed on something behind me. I wanted to turn, but my need to watch Adrian's reactions was greater. He looked bloodless. Petrified. I took a gamble. What had I to lose?

"I can stop this, Adrian. I can make it all go away. All you have to do is forgive her for placing the curse on you. Then she can pass over and you can find some kind of peace and—"

The pain struck me out of nowhere. I doubled over at the force of its stabbing, scything, gut-twisting agony. My breath came in short gasps. I felt as if I was being crushed between two heavy stones. An image of that black vapor I knew was Margarita swam in front of my eyes. I could feel it now, taking physical form, invading my body, controlling my nerve endings. Clawing upwards to my brain. It would do anything to stop me from persuading Adrian.

Through tear-filled eyes, I saw him stare in horror at me, then back to the apparition he must be seeing behind me.

He fled from the room, leaving the door wide open. I heard him thunder up the stairs before I passed out.

I came to in my room, with no recollection of getting there. Someone had placed a blanket over me to ward off the chill. Next to my bed was the ever-present bottle, although this time it would be filled purely with diluted brandy. I took a healthy swig. Despite the cold in the room, my body felt clammy and sweaty and my stomach was cramping. Not the awful pain from earlier, or my monthly period pains. This was something different, something that had me reaching for the bottle for another slug. Was I experiencing withdrawal symptoms from the laudanum? I hoped not. I couldn't afford to be incapacitated now.

I had to find Iris and get her out of this house. Determination helped me struggle to my feet and make my way down the darkened hallway. I had no idea of the time, only that it was late and, from the silence, I guessed everyone had gone to bed.

At the bottom of the stairs, I made my way to the door to the servants' hall and listened. Silence. I turned the handle. The door gave and I stepped in. A short landing led to a flight of stone stairs and I crept down. Only the light from an outside streetlamp and a full moon illuminated the room. I knew the servants slept upstairs in the attic, so there should be no sound. I listened again, hardly daring to breathe. Sure I had heard something. Maybe a mouse.

It came again. A slight whimper, as if someone was in pain. This time, I was certain it had come from beyond the hall. I had never been down here before and daren't light a candle, even supposing I could find one. In a minute, my eyes grew accustomed to my gloomy surroundings and I picked my way across the tidy room as the whimpering grew louder.

A tap dripped in the scullery. Then I heard the sound again. At the back was a closed door. I made my way towards it and turned the handle. Locked.

"Is there someone in there?" I called, my voice little more than a stage whisper.

Someone was in there, crying and in pain. "Iris, is that you?"

The whimpers turned to sobs.

I could have wept with her . "Oh, Iris, I'm so sorry. This is all my fault. I've come to get you away from here."

I peered through the gloom and then remembered. Iris had said Steddings kept the key to the French windows on a hook in his parlor. Surely he would keep the other keys there too. If only I could see clearly enough. There was nothing for it, I would have to get some light from somewhere. Then I saw a small row of candles in holders on the window sill, behind the sink.

I grabbed one and found the box of matches next to them. I struck a match and the flame burned into life. Shielding it with my free hand, I made my way out of the scullery and found another door, just off the servants' hall. I opened it, shone the candle around the walls and lit up a row of hooks. From each was suspended a key—each one labeled. I offered up a silent prayer of thanks and moved along the row, reading labels until I came across, "Scullery maid's bedroom". That had to be the one.

I unhooked the key and raced back to the door. My hands shook so much, I nearly dropped it, and I felt again a wave of sweat breaking out all over my body. I shivered and my head throbbed—another withdrawal symptom— but I had to ignore it.

In the flickering candlelight, I gasped at what I saw. Iris, gagged and bound by her legs and arms to the iron bedstead, her face bloodied and her hair wild. Her eyes were like a frightened animal's.

I rushed to her side and tried to untie the bonds. "Oh, God, Iris. Who did this to you?"

I managed to free her from the gag and she spluttered and gasped for breath. "The master had Steddings do it. He beat me and hit me with a belt until I couldn't stand the pain any longer. I'm so sorry, madam. I told them where you were. I couldn't help myself. It hurt so much and then the master…he…"

I had freed her arms now and she pointed a shaking finger down her body.

I looked to where she was pointing and recoiled. Her dress was soiled and she lay in a pool of her own congealed blood.

"He did this to you? He *raped* you?"

I could hardly hear her. "Yes."

Tears sprang to my eyes. What sort of a monster was he? I had never met such a depraved and evil son of a bitch. I wanted to kill him, but right now my priority was to get Iris out of harm's way. And I hadn't a clue how to go about it.

"Iris, do you have any family? Anyone you could go to who would look after you?"

Awkwardly, the tortured girl rubbed her recently freed limbs.

"My family's in Glasgow, but there's too many of us. I can't go back there."

"Is there no one else at all? A friend perhaps?"

"They're throwing me out of here tomorrow. I'll be out on the streets with barely a stitch of clothing and no money. Oh, madam…"

I held her and rocked her in my arms while she sobbed. My anger against Adrian grew stronger by the second, as did my own feeling of wretchedness and sickness. The poor girl had soiled herself at some time during her ordeal and the stench turned my already queasy stomach.

She choked back sobs and pulled away. "Oh, madam, I'm sorry, you're not well, are you?"

"Don't worry about me, Iris. That's just the lack of laudanum. My body was growing too dependent on it and now it wants what it's not going to get. The most important thing is to get you out of here, to somewhere safe."

"I have an aunt in Dundee. I haven't seen her since I was little. She always sends me a birthday card and a letter every Christmas. But I'd have to go on the train and I have no money."

"Don't worry about that. Can you stand?"

"I think so."

"Good. Now I'm going to find you some clothes and let you have something you can sell tomorrow morning. Do you know where to get a good price?"

She nodded. "I've heard Mr. Steddings talk about a man in the New Town. He gives good prices for gold and silver."

"Right. Now wish me luck because I'll have to go back upstairs and pack some of my clothes for you. They'll be a bit big on you, but they should keep you going."

"Oh, madam, I couldn't. They're much too good—"

"Nonsense. Just keep your fingers crossed Mr. Devine doesn't wake up."

She gave a little whimper of fright and I squeezed her hand as reassuringly as my feverish body would allow.

I would need both hands, so I left the candle for Iris. I now concentrated hard on willing my cramping legs to move and trudged up the stairs. At the top, I held on to the wall for support as I crept past Adrian's closed door.

Once again, luck was on my side and five minutes later, I was stuffing three serviceable dresses, a coat, boots and underwear into a suitcase. All I had to do now was get it down the stairs to Iris. I prayed the girl had managed to get herself on her feet and cleaned up a bit, because I didn't know how much longer I could keep going. My head swam as I staggered down the stairs, gripping the suitcase with one hand and the stair rail with the other.

Iris was patting herself dry in the scullery, with a towel inadequate for the purpose. She looked battered in the dim light, but a world away from the terrified girl I had discovered.

"I'm so grateful, madam. After I let you down so badly."

"You did *not* let me down, Iris. I should never have put you in that position and I wouldn't if I hadn't been desperate."

"Was it worth it, madam? I mean, could your friend help?"

I nodded. "Now, I'm going to get something for you to sell. I'll be back as soon as I can. Grab some clothes out of the suitcase and get dressed and then we'll get you out of here."

As I crossed the hall, the clock chimed and I nearly fell over at the sudden noise, but I plowed on, bathed in sweat. Every muscle, every bone in my body ached and I craved the little blue bottle. Even brandy alone would take off the edge.

I pressed my ear against the closed drawing room door. No sign of light but, even though I was sure Adrian was safely upstairs in bed, I still took precious seconds opening it quietly.

Moonlight shone into the room, and I knew exactly what to take. Two silver candlesticks and a small, but heavy, trinket box. Adrian would probably miss them straight away, but then he would also know Iris had escaped and only one person in this house would be brave, or stupid, enough to help her. By now, I felt too ill to care what else he did to me. I just had to get Iris out of there.

My hand ached to reach for the decanter of brandy, but, somehow, I resisted and made my way back to Iris, my arms full of my trophies. I paused in the hall to listen for any sound. There wasn't any. Just the ticking of the clock.

Sweat dripped off my nose. I felt nauseous and my head swam, but I struggled back to the scullery, to find Iris dressed. She looked almost normal, except for the bruising on her face and a split lip.

She managed a smile that quickly turned to horror as she saw me more clearly.

"Oh, madam, you look awful. You need to see a doctor."

"Never mind me," I said as I thrust the silverware into her hands. "Stick these in the suitcase and let's get you out of here."

She did as I prompted. Then she produced a key from the draining board. "I got this from Mr. Steddings's parlor. It opens the servants' door down here."

"Good. Come on, there's no time to lose. The clock struck four as I was going to the drawing room."

"Sarah will be up in about an hour."

"Ready?" I steadied myself by holding on to the sink.

Iris nodded and, in an impulsive gesture, hugged me. "I'll never be able to thank you enough."

"Nor I you, Iris. Just go and have a wonderful life. A lot's going to happen in your lifetime. Keep yourself safe."

She unlocked the door and handed me the key. Then, a quick smile and she was gone into the freezing darkness.

I locked the door and my fingers ached so much I could hardly make them turn the key. Ten minutes later, I was back in bed, fully clothed, shivering too much to undress. I was freezing and my limbs spasmed without mercy. Every time I slipped into merciful oblivion, a searing leg cramp would drag me awake and send me screaming in agony.

Darkness became dawn, then daylight.

I was vaguely aware of Adrian at one point. He looked down on me, anger all over his face but, seeing my distress, he smiled. Then he moved away, or maybe I imagined it.

Daylight became dusk, then darkness again.

No one else came. Perhaps Adrian was waiting for this cold turkey to tip me over the edge before he called the asylum, or maybe this was my punishment, to be left to rot in my own bodily fluids. I vomited bile, my bowels shut down and awful hallucinations of giant insects crawled over me.

My skin itched until I was frantically dragging myself around the room, trying to escape it. Then more insects crawled down the walls, their pincers snapping and chewing, like massive green and blue spiders, morphed with cockroaches.

Then, at last, the convulsions grew less frequent, the cramps less agonizing and, finally, I slept, on the floor now, as far away from my own mess as possible, even though my body must be caked in it.

I had no idea how long I had been asleep, but when I woke up, my head pounded and my stench assaulted my nostrils. But at least I was alive and the room didn't swim before my eyes or reveal disgusting creatures I knew couldn't be there.

I hoisted myself to my feet, with the help of a nearby chair. Then I hobbled over to the wardrobe and opened it. I took down my dressing gown and limped to the bathroom. Daylight, but on which day? Maybe Adrian was at home or maybe at work. I neither knew nor, at that moment, cared. All I wanted was a bath, and never to return to that stinking bedroom ever again.

I was thankful for the luxury of hot running water as I scrubbed off the muck and soaped myself. I changed the water and, this time, sank into its restoring embrace.

As I lay back, I thought over what I needed to do. I dreaded the inevitable confrontation over Iris but, after my recent ordeal, what more could Adrian do to hurt me? There was no doubt, the urgency to get him to forgive Grace had cranked up a notch. If he intended to commit me, I must have provided him with enough evidence by now. He could be drawing up the papers at that very moment.

I clambered out of the bath and patted myself dry before slipping on the robe. I opened the wardrobe in the filthy bedroom, and took out a loose fitting gown. Then, I tied my rapidly drying hair back into a pony tail and examined my appearance in the mirror. At last. My own reflection. But I had become so gaunt. My eyes were hollow and round, with dark circles underneath them. I looked for all the world like my specter.

Was the withdrawal over? I prayed so. I would need all the strength I could muster for what I had to do.

Chapter Sixteen

I wasn't prepared for the sight that greeted me when I pushed open the drawing room door.

Adrian didn't seem to notice my arrival. He stood, immobile, by the fireplace, transfixed by something in the far corner of the room.

I followed his gaze and gasped.

Grace floated just above the floor, dressed in her usual white, floral flecked dress, holding her hat in one hand. This time though, she was surrounded by a shimmering halo of silvery white. She gazed out at Adrian, a pleading look in her eyes. I looked back at him and noticed his hand was trembling. He was in profile, but what I could see of his face was deathly pale.

I felt something wriggling inside me. As if I'd swallowed some small animal, now desperate to escape. It clawed and clutched my stomach and I doubled over. I thought for a moment the withdrawal was back, but then I gagged. Something forced its way up my throat— vile tasting. Slimy. It pushed its way into my mouth and I retched. I could barely breathe. A thick, black, glistening worm slithered out of my mouth and dropped to the carpet. It stank of excrement. I stared at it, unable to believe such a disgusting thing had come out of me. A jug of water and a tumbler stood on a nearby table and I reached for them, splashed water into the glass and drank it down, then another, and another until, finally, I was rid of the awful taste. My stomach muscles heaved again and I vomited bile.

All the while, I never took my eyes of the slithering creature that now wriggled its hideous way towards Grace's apparition. In those few seconds it had doubled its size. Neither she nor Adrian seemed to see it. Neither had reacted to my presence, as if I wasn't even there. As I watched, the creature began to change and slowly grew a torso, then arms and legs. It was jet black and face down, but it resembled a human.

Then it got to its feet and I backed away. It slowly turned towards me, its metamorphosis complete. Margarita. She widened her mouth in a parody of a grin, her eyes black, her remaining flesh crawling with maggots. Worst of all, I realized she'd been lying dormant inside me for days, all through my ordeals, maybe even orchestrating them.

I screamed and backed off. Still, Adrian and Grace ignored me.

"They can't see or hear you," Margarita said. "I am ready to bargain. You wish to save the girl's soul, to send her to the light?"

I swallowed hard. My voice came out as a whisper. "Yes."

"She is nothing to me. My son is everything. Do you understand?"

I nodded.

"You have a decision to make, while we are here, suspended in time."

My heart pounded and my palms broke into a cold sweat.

"I will persuade my son to forgive the girl. He will do as I ask. He knows better than to refuse me. In so doing though, his life, both now and in your time, will end and his soul will return with me."

I stared at her. I knew where she would take him.

"We will be together. Not as he would have wished. I gave him everlasting life in this world, but now you have brought her here, this can no longer be."

Finally, the jigsaw was complete. "If Adrian forgives Grace, he will show mercy, and that is the one quality that would break his bond with you forever, isn't it? You want him with you, no matter what the cost to his soul, because yours is already damned forever."

Her expression told me I was right. "Just take my offer and we can all be done with this."

There had to be a price. I sensed with Margarita, there was always a price. Even for her own son. "What do you want in return?"

I was rewarded with the hideous grin. "Maybe nothing. Maybe something. Perhaps today, tomorrow or never. It is the risk you take."

"But I need something more concrete than that. Are you bargaining for my soul? Will I be damned to some kind of everlasting hell on earth?"

"How strong is your spirit? Many spirits survive. Are you strong enough to trust yours?"

What kind of a question was that? How could I possibly know? Yet, at least she was saying I had a chance of making everything right—as long as my spirit was able to reject whatever evil might try and attack it. And, of course, as long as I could trust that she was telling me the truth. Right now, that was a pretty big task, but also the only conceivable way out of this horror.

We stood there, locked in that time warp, in the room, but not a part of it. Could I persuade Adrian without her intervention? If so, then Grace could move on and I wouldn't have to take any gambles with my own soul.

But one look at Margarita and I knew she would never let that happen. She had to be in control and wherever she had come from originally, she was hell's champion now.

"You won't let me leave this…this limbo, will you?"

Still grinning, she slowly shook her mantilla-shrouded head. "As you would say, we have all the time in the world, and no time may pass at all."

Whatever *that* meant.

I lost track of time, assuming there was any in that place. We were like statues, and, while Grace's apparition still shimmered, Adrian stood, like some marble sculpture, frozen in fear.

What choice did I have? I had exhausted all my options, not that there had been many to begin with.

"Very well," I said at last. "I trust my spirit to withstand whatever you may, or may not, decide to throw at it. It's brought me this far anyway, so it can't be too weak."

The grin broadened. She faded. I still stood in the same spot, but now Adrian saw me for the first time since I'd entered that room.

He didn't shout, remonstrate or make any attempt to strike me. He just stared, and I'm sure his eyes held more questions than he could put into words. But I wasn't concerned with him now.

Had Margarita kept her promise? Would Adrian now forgive his stepsister for the curse he had so richly deserved, but which had cost her eternal peace?

Grace's apparition stopped shimmering. She stood in front of us, more solid than I had ever seen her. I managed a weak smile and she smiled back. Her face lit up and I knew she sensed something.

I looked from her to Adrian. "Do you have something to say to Grace?"

He nodded slowly and turned back to her. When he spoke, his voice echoed as if in an empty hall. "I...forgive...you."

A shape slowly emerged next to Grace. My specter. I watched in amazement as Grace smiled at me and then at the figure I had known for so long, but had never seen clearly. Now, she appeared from behind her hollow-eyed mask. She embraced the young girl and then I recognized her from her photograph. Agnes, Grace's mother. I watched them embrace. I opened my mouth, but could find no words.

Then I had to shield my eyes from the bright light that filled the room. I lost track of Adrian, but suddenly Grace stood at my side. She touched my arm and warmth flowed through me.

Tears streamed from my eyes. "Rest in peace, Grace. You can go over now."

I watched her, even though the light stung my eyes. Steered by her mother's loving embrace, she moved into the brightness. As the two figures receded from sight, the light dimmed in the room and then faded altogether.

I caught a last glimpse of Adrian. His face became a mask of horror as he realized his mother's treachery. His screams tore through me. Maybe I could have pitied him if he had ever shown any pity for anyone else. Instead, I just watched as he disappeared into the gaping jaws of hell. In that maelstrom, his unnatural mother waited to possess him forever.

Everything around me swirled and I fell deeper and deeper. My stomach lurched once. Then I woke up.

I was lying on the chaise longue, but straightaway I knew something had changed. I looked down at myself, dressed in my familiar jeans and top. My trainers felt strange and comfortable after months in horribly tight shoes and boots. I stood up and couldn't believe how recharged and full of life I felt.

I was still in Adrian Devine's house, the furnishings little changed from the 1912 version. Now that Grace was at peace, I just wanted to get out of there. I caught sight of myself in the mirror and was relieved to see that the gaunt and haunted look had left me. My hair was a little mussed but apart from that, no one would ever guess what I'd been through.

But my reflection wasn't the only person in the mirror. I spun around to see Martyn Devine slumped in his chair, his mouth open and his face gray. His hands gripped the arms of the Chesterfield and I knew, without any doubt, that he was dead.

But I had to be sure. I took one reluctant step after another and reached out to touch his neck. I felt for a pulse. His skin felt cold, dry as a withered autumn leaf and he must have been dead for some time.

I should call for an ambulance. A bit late for that, but someone would have to sign the death certificate. How on earth would I explain my presence? How would I explain anything about this man? I just wanted to get the hell out of there and back to Greg. One look at my watch, now safely back on my wrist, told me a quarter of an hour had elapsed since I'd arrived, assuming it was still the same day. The trees were coming into leaf, I could see them out of the window, so it definitely wasn't the November I had left behind in 1912. Maybe Greg hadn't missed me at all because I'd only been gone an hour or so.

My handbag lay on the chaise longue. I grabbed it and fished around for my phone. My hands closed on the familiar rectangle of plastic and glass.

I flicked it on and saw the battery, still fully charged. That answered my question. This had to be the same day. With no more hesitation, I dialed '999' and fifteen minutes later the police arrived, followed by an ambulance. I had already decided on my story.

My name was Meredith James and I was researching my novel, loosely based on the Devine family. I had arranged a meeting to interview Adrian Devine's son. When I had arrived, I'd found the door slightly open. I'd come in, found Mr. Devine dead in his chair and rung them.

The young police officer put away his notebook, while the paramedics laid the dead man on a stretcher and covered his face with a blanket. My last sight of Martyn Devine unnerved me. Lying there in death, he should have looked peaceful, but his open mouth, which rigor mortis prevented from closing, seemed to have been caught in a scream. The man looked as if he had died of fright. Had he too joined his father in hell? Or had he just witnessed it somehow? I turned away. Sickened.

Greg looked up from his reading and smiled as I bounded into our room.

"Had a good morning?"

I didn't answer, but he didn't know what had hit him when I raced up to him and threw my arms around him.

He dropped his papers and laughed. "Hey, what's all this? I only saw you at breakfast."

"Are you sure?" I asked and then caught the confused frown. "Oh, it doesn't matter. Of course you did. But I can miss you, can't I?"

The fervent kisses led to more and half an hour later, we were snuggled in bed, content and satiated.

"I think this holiday's been good for us. Strange, but good," Greg said, squeezing me tighter.

"Definitely strange," I said.

"Why is it I keep getting the feeling I'm missing something? That you've been having a totally different experience to mine?"

"Probably because I have," I replied as I kissed his fingers in turn. "I've been researching the Devine family and you've been working. As usual."

"I've taken some time off."

"Okay." I sat up in bed. "Look, we only have a couple of days left. Why don't we spend them together, just rambling around Edinburgh, sightseeing? Maybe we could visit the Royal Yacht Britannia. I've always wanted to."

"You're on, but this afternoon, I just need to spend half an hour reading through a report one of my clients has sent me. He wants me to give it the once over before he delivers it to a large prospective customer of his."

"Will you need your laptop?"

"No. Not until I email him with my thoughts. Want to borrow it for twenty minutes or so?"

"Yes, please. Then I'll have a shower while you do your email."

"I'll follow you."

That would give me the opportunity to check the painting in the wardrobe. I wanted to see if it had changed.

On Greg's laptop I searched for any information on Louisa Mayhew. There were quite a few links and I quickly eliminated one after the other, until a white-haired, old lady stared out at me. I clicked on to it and found it was a family page.

There were other photographs and there was no mistaking the younger Louisa. I read that she had never remarried but had gone on to open her own exclusive dress shop for fashionable Edinburgh ladies. Her children had both lived in Edinburgh until after her death in 1953, at the age of eighty-two. The page had been started by one of her seven grandchildren and it seemed that all her descendants now lived in the USA, scattered through seven states from Rhode Island in the east to California in the west.

I bookmarked the page. Maybe one day I would get up the courage to email the contact there. I would love to hear more about his grandmother's later life.

Of Iris, whose surname, I knew, was McKenzie, I could find no trace. I just hoped and prayed she had made a happy life for herself. Maybe she had married and changed her name? I would never know.

Then I searched for Mayhew and Sons. A brief entry appeared for the brewery, which had been absorbed by a large conglomerate in 1963. The last owner was Martyn Devine, who was "appointed by his father", although Adrian's actual name wasn't recorded. Then as a seemingly unrelated footnote, I read, "Charlotte Devine, mother of

Martyn, died April 16th, 1912." The same day I had slipped back in time. Murder? Or a convenient coincidence? Whatever the answer, I was sure Adrian was, somehow, responsible. Well, he was paying the price now.

I closed the laptop.

"Finished?" Greg asked.

"For now. I'll go and get that shower."

The warm spray soothed me and the ordeal of the last six months faded further into the distance. I suppose it was my mind's way of coping with the incongruity of what I'd lived through. Before long, even I would wonder if it had ever happened. But then, events would have a way of reminding me it really had.

I emerged from the shower, refreshed and cleansed, a towel wrapped around me.

"Perfect timing," Greg said and kissed my nose as he passed me on his way to the bathroom.

As soon as he shut the door and I heard the shower start, I opened the wardrobe, reached up and found what I was looking for.

I stared at the rolled-up canvas. What if it was still the same? But then I reminded myself, nothing remained constant where this picture was concerned. Of course it would be different. But, in what way?

I took a deep breath and unrolled it.

The familiar blue-green water came into view. The canvas felt dry this time. Just like any other oil painting.

I held it out in front of me and stared at it.

The picture was just a mass of blue-green opaque water. Grace had gone. Then I caught sight of something in the bottom left-hand corner I had never seen before. A signature. I'd searched every inch of that painting trying to find who painted it. Now I knew.

In very small letters, the painting was signed 'A. Devine'.

There was no date.

Chapter Seventeen

In the end, I packed up the picture and handed it over at the Post Office in a town thirty miles away from my home. Duncan would receive an anonymous donation of a nondescript painting of lake water. The last time I looked, the signature was still there, so it would make an interesting curiosity if nothing else.

I didn't call him until two days after we returned. He had already left three messages for me on my phone, but it took me that long to decide how much to tell him. In the end, I decided to say very little. He needn't know about the timeslip. Only that Grace had been forgiven and had passed over.

He was clearly relieved. "I became quite worried when I didn't hear from you."

"Oh, there's no need. I'm fine. I'm really sorry I didn't return your calls. My phone's been acting up. Turns out my SIM card had slipped out of kilter and it's taken me days to work it out. I didn't even know you'd called." Still the lies toppled out.

"Not to worry. You're safe and sound and home again. I do hope you'll come back one day and visit."

"I'd like that," I said, knowing I would never go back. The mere thought of Arnsay and I shuddered. "Has anything been happening since we last spoke?"

"No, it's been quiet. I even switched the CCTV on again upstairs and monitored it. There have been no manifestations and no customers scurrying out of the museum. I think you laid all the ghosts to rest when you went to see Martyn Devine."

"I'd like to think so. I saw his death made the news."

"Yes, they said a young woman called Meredith James found him. It seems to have been around the time you visited him too. Was he all right when you left him?"

"Yes. Well, he was as doddery and vague as before, and, of course, he was ancient."

"That Meredith James seems to have disappeared as well. The newspapers have been trying to trace her, but apparently she gave the police a false address. Of course, there was no foul play so they aren't concerned, but it is odd, don't you think? I mean, why would she just disappear? She'd done nothing wrong."

"Probably just didn't want to get involved. You know how people are." My palms were sweating now.

"You're probably right." His voice held more than a note of suspicion, but as long as I refused to admit anything, that's just what it would remain.

Not long after that, we wished each other well and I hung up.

More searches on the Internet had revealed nothing concerning Martyn Devine before his death, now there were pages and pages devoted to the old man who had lived on his own for as long as anyone could remember. Neighbors said they had never seen him. He never ventured out and had everything—meals included—delivered to his door.

A few days later, Duncan's picture began to appear and the connection between the old man and the island of Arnsay made for an interesting story.

Fourteen months later, Duncan had evidently found himself an agent because he was the darling of the Sunday supplements, with a book in the offing. The story of Grace and her step-family was about to be published.

Good luck to him, I thought, until the day I opened the Sunday newspaper to find myself staring at a photograph of Margarita.

My stomach lurched. I dropped the newspaper as a sudden rush of heat spread through my body, burning and stinging. My head swam and sweat broke out all over me. My arms glistened. I could feel trickles of it running down my face, only to fall in droplets, where it stained my blue T-shirt.

I was glad Greg was out, visiting a client. I had roughly two hours to pull myself together.

Fifteen uneventful months had gone by since that fateful holiday, during which the fear of Margarita's threat had faded into oblivion. I had reached the point where I no longer believed her ability to exact a price for her help. Now all my fears rushed back.

My stomach lurched, as if something had woken up and was moving around inside me. I panicked. Something must have lain dormant in my body all this time. Something Margarita had bequeathed me. She didn't like what Duncan was doing and I would have to pay the price for it. My temperature shot up. Sweat broke out all over my body.

I plunged my face into a bowl of freezing cold water in the bathroom. When I came up for air, gasping and choking, my body still burned with an unnatural fire.

I toweled my face dry and gazed at my reflection in the mirror. A stranger stared back at me. Oh, I looked like me, but my eyes were different. The same color as usual, the same shape as usual, but they saw the world in a different way. I was seeing with Margarita's eyes.

Anger twisted itself around my spine. All consuming, passionate, full of hate. I couldn't bear it any longer and raced out of the bathroom. I threw myself on the bed, sobbing and shaking. A cacophony of shrieks and moans filled my head and I tore at my hair, trying to release my demons. I screamed, yelled myself hoarse.

And then, suddenly, they were gone. It was all gone. I dared to look at my reflection in the dressing table mirror and the relief was like a tsunami. My eyes looked out on the world again, but I now had a job I must do.

My hair made me look like a scarecrow and my clothes were wringing wet. I changed everything, underwear included, brushed my tangled hair and applied make up. Then I picked up the phone.

"Duncan? It's Alex Fletcher. I need to talk to you about the book you're due to publish soon."

"Alex, how lovely to hear from you. You just caught me. I'm packing up as we speak. I'm off to London for a few weeks to promote it. Isn't it great news? Grace's story will finally be told, although whether anyone will believe the ending remains to be seen."

I took a deep breath. This was going to be so hard for him to hear and he would probably think I was insane.

"Duncan, please listen to me. It's very important. You can't publish it."

A momentary pause. Then, "I beg your pardon? Can't publish it? Why? I thought you wanted to tell Grace's story. When you clearly weren't doing so, I went ahead—"

"No, Duncan, it's not that I have a book planned. None of us can publish that story."

"Whyever not?"

"I realize now I should have told you everything about my visit to Martyn Devine. It's all to do with Adrian's mother."

"Margarita? She's featured in the book quite a bit. I believe she was instrumental in the development of Adrian's sociopathic nature."

"Oh, I have no doubt about it. And that's the reason you can't publish. She doesn't want you to and, believe me, I have no idea how much she can do to you, but she is already tormenting me. If I don't stop this publication, she will call in the debt I owe her. She persuaded Adrian to forgive Grace."

His voice sounded confused, faraway, as if trying to make sense of what I'd said, and failing. "I don't understand any of that."

"Duncan, I know you don't. I have to ask you to trust me. Margarita is the very definition of evil and she embedded a part of herself in me, like some sort of sleeper. You know, what they used to call spies during the Cold War?"

"I know what a sleeper is, Alex, but it's the rest of it that doesn't make sense. Margarita has been dead for over a century. What really happened during your visit to Martyn Devine? I mean, you couldn't have been there long."

I took a deep breath. Now I had to tell him. And I did so. Every last detail, even including the debt I now owed to Margarita. He needed to know everything if I was ever to have a chance of dissuading him from publishing. All the time I spoke, I heard a succession of disbelieving gasps from the other end of the phone.

He let me finish and I held my breath.

His words were not encouraging, "Alex, please. I'm open-minded, you know that. I've seen and experienced things here that scared the life out of me. But this is too much, even for me. I really think you got too caught up in this whole thing. I mean, for a start, you weren't away more than a few hours at most, were you? Certainly not six months. Your husband would have been frantic and you would have been plastered all over the papers as a missing person."

"I'm not a scientist. I can't explain it, but somehow I slipped through time."

"Into a parallel universe?'

Was he mocking me? Maybe he thought I was mocking him.

"Frankly, I don't know, but when I came to, I was back in that house and virtually no time had elapsed. Except that Martyn was now dead, of course."

The words were out before I had thought through their impact.

"So it *was* you. *You* were Meredith James. I *knew* it. You lied to me, Alex." He sounded disappointed and betrayed. Why hadn't I confided in him?

"I know and I'm so sorry, Duncan. I just didn't want to involve you and that's why I didn't tell you all this before. I never thought I'd need to. And it can all stop. All you have to do is withdraw from your contract and cancel the book. I know it's a big ask but—"

"It's too late."

"*What?*" My head pounded.

"It's too late. *Laying Ghosts to Rest* was published this morning. Because of the interest generated over Martyn's death and my agent's hard work promoting me and the story, the publisher had healthy advance orders. I understand it'll be in the shops today. I'm sorry, Alex, but even if I wanted to, I couldn't stop it." He sighed and it felt as if a gust of wind had blown in my ear. "Maybe it's best if we don't call each other again. I'm a bit upset about this and it should be the happiest day of my life."

"I'm so sorry, Duncan. I really am."

The phone went dead.

I sank down onto the living room settee and put my head in my hands. What was I going to do? Margarita wouldn't leave me alone. Sooner or later she would be back and she would want something. She would stop at nothing to get it, of that I was sure. And I would be her unwilling accomplice.

"Are you okay, Alex? You look pale."

I managed a wobbly smile at Greg and carried on cutting up carrots for our dinner. "Just a bit tired, that's all. I didn't have a particularly good night. Kept waking up."

"Probably the heat. It's been airless these past few nights."

I nodded and pushed a lock of damp hair out of my eye. I had become hot all of a sudden and it bothered me.

Kill him…kill him…kill him…

I dropped the knife as if it had burned me and stared at my hand.

Greg retrieved it from the floor, washed it and handed it back to me. I daren't take it from him. I stared at it as I rubbed my burning hand. I had an almost overwhelming desire to plunge that knife into Greg's heart.

I burst into tears and fled the kitchen, into the bedroom and threw myself on the bed.

Greg was there in an instant. He tried to hold me, but I pushed him away, too scared of what I might do.

"Please don't touch me," I said.

"Why ever not? Alex, what's wrong? Christ, you're burning up. I'm calling the doctor."

I tried to stop him, but gave up. Let a doctor examine me. Perhaps, with luck, they'd find something, give me some pills. Make it go away.

But I knew my wish was in vain. No cure had yet been discovered for what was wrong with me. Demonic possession? Take three pills, four times a day with a glass of water and avoid alcohol. If only.

———

In any event, the doctor prescribed a couple of weeks' rest. Rest! The state my mind was in, rest was the last thing I was capable of. He told Greg and me that, in his considered opinion, I was run down. Losing my job had been a highly stressful experience, rather like losing a loved one. He said I was still grieving, even after all this time.

Greg listened, nodded and took it all in, then promptly wrapped me in cotton wool and pampered me. It only added to my feelings of guilt. I didn't deserve such a good man. Not when my heart was becoming blackened and evil. Irrational, murderous thoughts would spring into my mind from nowhere, with no warning.

I became frightened to go shopping, after I narrowly escaped being arrested for aggravated assault. *Me*, for heaven's sake. In an argument over the last supermarket trolley!

But then, it wasn't me, was it? Those outbursts might look like me, talk like me, use my body, but Margarita and I both knew it was her seed, no longer sleeping, but growing. Soon, if unchecked, it would take me over altogether. I couldn't let that happen.

I watched Greg grow increasingly absentminded and knew it was my fault. He was consumed with worry over me and tried to persuade me to see a psychiatrist, but I refused.

I spent much of my time going over the events of that momentous April, the next six months of my life that I apparently hadn't lived, and the belief that I had found the answer to why Grace's mother—my specter—had hovered over Greg, as well as me, at the stone circle. She knew he was in danger. I also believed that the reason she had told me to leave the circle was that she sensed another presence there. Margarita. You can work a lot of things out when all you have is time on your hands. The only remaining conundrum was why Grace had chosen me in the first place. She'd said I was the only one who would truly listen to her, but was that really the only reason? I became increasingly bothered by a coincidence. My grandmother had been born on the very day Grace had died. I had heard of the spirits of the newly dead mingling with those of the newborn. Maybe here lay another, less random connection. After all, Grandma had given my mother Grace's name.

Then one night, as I tried to sleep, a long-forgotten memory floated back into my mind. Me, at four years old. My grandmother giving me a pretty white dress, with little flowers on it, for my birthday. "Now all you need is a bright red coat," she had said.

But my mother wouldn't buy me one. I never knew why.

One Saturday evening, Greg insisted we went out to dinner to celebrate our anniversary.

"We haven't been anywhere since we got back from Edinburgh and that was months ago. I'll book us a table at Riverina's. You know how you love their pasta."

I hesitated. I didn't feel as tired today. The strange, irrational and frightening urges had been quiet for a few days. Maybe it would do me good to get out and about.

Since the shopping incident, which I'd managed to keep from Greg, I had taken to ordering household supplies and food to be delivered. I hardly set foot outside the house and garden, and the promised novel had long since been abandoned. My days were spent mostly fighting myself. I'd find myself staring off into space. I'd lose track of time and then snap back to find half an hour—or even longer—had elapsed. I'd just zapped out somehow. Fortunately it didn't happen when Greg was there, just when I was alone, with nothing to do.

I made my decision. "That would be lovely, Greg. Thank you."

He made no attempt to conceal the sigh of relief. "For a moment there, I thought you were going to turn me down again." He put his arms around me and I let him draw me close. He smelled warm and familiar and it soothed me.

"I miss you, Alex," he whispered. "Come back to me. Please."

I lifted my head up to look into his eyes, too quickly for him to change his expression and, for a second, I saw desperation and sadness there. Then his smile returned and I smiled too. We both kept our fears to ourselves these days.

Riverina's had been our favorite restaurant for almost as long as we had been together. It had been the first place Greg had taken me for a meal and I'd fallen in love with Alfredo's divine pasta dishes.

Cannelloni, lasagna, fusilli, even the Bolognese was different than any I had ever tasted before. And that included our two trips to Venice.

As usual he greeted us like long lost friends, planted a kiss on both my cheeks and shook Greg's hand warmly. A wide grin stretched from ear to ear.

"Welcome, welcome, my friends. It has been a long time since we see you. I think you are deserting us. Maybe going to Ronaldo's." He shook his head. Ronaldo's was on the other side of town and had a one-star rating on TripAdvisor, in contrast to Riverina's five stars.

"As if we would, Alfredo. You know we can't resist your food," Greg said. "We've just been really busy that's all, but we're back now, aren't we, Alex?"

"Yes," I replied, trying to sound more certain than I felt. Already, I felt an uncomfortable stirring in the pit of my stomach and I prayed I'd get through this evening without a problem.

The first course went off without a hitch and, as we waited for the entrées, Greg poured our favorite Barolo. The wine slid down my throat—velvety smooth, full bodied and rich.

"You look lovely tonight, Alex. Happy anniversary. Eleven years together. Where has all the time gone?"

I shook my head and we clinked glasses. Greg sighed. "I do love you, you know. I hope you realize that."

"I know," I said and a heady cocktail of guilt, sadness and love welled up inside me. "I love you too. More than I can say."

I realized my right hand was fiddling with the steak knife that lay in anticipation of Steak Rossini. Involuntarily, I tightened my grip on it and held it like a dagger.

Kill him… kill him…kill him…

I threw down the knife with a cry, shoved back my chair and backed straight into the waiter who was carrying our meals. He fell back and landed on the next table—a party of four, enjoying their desserts.

Without waiting to apologize and knowing I could never explain my actions, I raced out of the restaurant, into the sultry evening air, where I leaned against the wall, panting.

Greg joined me a few minutes later. "What the hell happened back there? You do realize we'll never be able to set foot in there again, don't you?"

I burst into hysterical sobs. "I'm so sorry, Greg. So sorry."

His anger must have turned to concern because he held me close and put his arm around me as he led me, still sobbing to the car. The only sound on our journey home came from me, trying to stem my tears and failing miserably.

Chapter Eighteen

We drifted and became like strangers after that.

I didn't want it that way, of course. I wanted to hold him close and tell him what was wrong. A battle raged for control within me. I had to force myself not to cry out with the force of it, as it tore me apart as surely as if someone was stabbing me constantly, day after day. I would catch Greg looking at me, as if he too was trying to weed out the cause of my increasingly odd behavior.

I suppose it was inevitable that someone like Judy would come along—and that I would find out about her.

Not that I blamed him. Why shouldn't he find solace elsewhere? I had managed to ruin both our lives. He didn't dare take me out anywhere and I was unemployable. My mood swings were so outrageous. He had come home one day to find the dining room curtains in shreds because I couldn't get them off their hooks to wash them. He had to prepare all the meals because of my fear of sharp knives. I didn't tell him that every time I got one in my hand, Margarita's voice would start its deadly, hypnotic chant.

Kill him…kill him…kill him…

My doctor referred me to a psychiatrist and I pretended to go. Every Thursday at ten o'clock I would leave the house and walk to the bus stop, even if Greg wasn't at home. Just in case one of the neighbors saw me and mentioned anything to him.

I traveled into town, got off the bus and wandered around the shops for an hour. I never bought anything. I didn't want anything.

Nothing mattered anymore. Then I got back on the bus and came home. My only journey of the week.

The discovery that I was no longer the only woman in Greg's life came by chance during a rare bit of housework. A pile of Greg's papers fell onto the floor and, as I retrieved them, a Valentine's card fell out of a file. It was now the end of March, and I knew I hadn't sent him one. My mind was too full of its own struggles to remember anniversaries or significant dates.

A big red heart adorned the front. Inside, just one word, 'Judy', followed by a collection of kisses and a couple of hand drawn hearts. I stared at it for at least five minutes as my heart pounded and my head began to throb.

A year ago, the idea of an unfaithful Greg would have been unthinkable. Since that bloody book was published and Margarita had decided to call in her favor, everything had changed.

To his credit, he didn't attempt to deny it. He cried. "I'm so sorry, Alex. I know it's wrong. I was just so lonely."

I amazed myself with how calm I felt. "Do you love her?"

He shook his head.

"Does she love you?"

"I don't know. Maybe. It's more of a friendship than anything. She's one of my clients."

"I guessed as much. A friendship with benefits I imagine?"

"I'm not going to deny it. I can't even remember the last time you and I made love, and I miss the closeness. You're like a stranger these days." He sighed. "Not that it excuses my behavior. It doesn't. I'm so sorry."

He tried to touch me but I backed away, more shocked by my feelings than his behavior, but I didn't want him to know that. In that moment I realized I had lost all self-respect. I didn't deserve to be loved. Greg did.

"Do you want a divorce?" I asked, still calm.

He shook his head. "I want you to get better. I don't think this psychiatrist is helping. If anything, you seem to be getting worse."

"I don't go there."

His expression changed from guilt and sadness to incredulity. "What?"

"I don't go there. It's a waste of time. He can't help me. No one can."

He wouldn't let me shrug him off this time. He gripped my arms and I could tell he was fighting back anger.

"Alex, listen to me. You have to get help. You're not well and if you refuse to go voluntarily, I shall have to get you committed. I honestly believe you're a danger to yourself and possibly to others."

I stared at him. So it had come to this, after all. "You'd put me in an asylum?"

"There aren't any asylums these days. Just hospitals where you would receive specialist care."

"There are no specialists for what I have wrong with me."

"I'm sure lots of people in your situation say the same thing."

"You don't understand." My tears flowed. They did so often these days. "Alex, darling, let me help you."

This time, I sank to the floor and sobbed so hard I could barely breathe.

Greg knelt down in front of me and drew me close. "You're having a mental breakdown and you need help. I'm not messing about any longer."

Kill him…kill him…kill him…

"*No!*" I wrenched myself out of his embrace and scrambled to my feet. My left hand trembled, while my right hand no longer felt connected to me. I grabbed it with my left, feeling the flesh and bone beneath my fingers. I massaged it but, as I did so, I had the weird sensation of clutching someone else's hand.

Greg grabbed his phone off his desk and I backed against the wall.

He made a brief call, but I couldn't hear what he said. A loud hissing echoed in my ears and blocked off all other sound. I lost track of myself and of time. At some stage, two pairs of strong arms almost lifted me off my feet. I remember the inside of the ambulance, and I remember the place they took me to.

A smiling female psychiatrist assessed me. She called it by some fancy name but, in translation, it amounted to a total mental breakdown. I was to be admitted, treated. They didn't know how long I would be there. It all depended on me. If I was a good girl, did what I was told, took my medication and followed all their instructions, I could be out in a month. If I failed on even one of these measures, I would remain there indefinitely. Until I was cured.

All that time, Margarita left me alone. She was patient, that one.

Greg visited me every day. Neither he nor I mentioned Judy and I had no idea if she was still in his life. I told myself it was all my only fault anyway and I had no right to question him.

I concentrated on remaining calm and well behaved in my therapy sessions. I knew my doctor realized I was holding something back but, however much she probed and prompted, I never once told her about Margarita, Grace or any of it. I knew if I did, I would probably never get out of there.

Finally, after three weeks, she gave up. While she wouldn't use the word 'cured', she did say I could go home, along with all my drugs. I must attend for weekly therapy for the time being and I had a list of instructions a yard long.

The first week passed smoothly. Margarita still left me alone and now, when Greg tried to touch me, or kiss me, I didn't pull away. We made love for the first time in months and it was so good, we did it again...and again. By now, I knew Judy must be history.

I started preparing the meals again, grateful that I could once again pick up a sharp knife without that nagging voice egging me on to commit murder. Why did she want Greg dead anyway? That had puzzled me for a long time, until I realized. It wouldn't matter who it was. She didn't care. She wanted me to kill someone—anyone— because then my soul would be as damned as hers.

Spring brought sunny days, fresh green leaves and birdsong. May saw the magnolias in full bloom, while wild cherry and apple blossom festooned the trees in our road. I started getting out more.

Greg even dared to take me to dinner, but not to Riverina's. We found a new place with excellent Mediterranean food. I can almost taste their delicious moussaka now.

I started gardening in earnest and planted pansies, violas and begonias. Their vivid colors cheered me and I started to feel alive again.

A year passed and another spring brought brilliant news. I'd found a publisher for that novel I finally wrote. I had abandoned any thoughts of writing about Grace and had kept to much safer territory—a romance about finding love in middle age. Greg and I danced around the room when I read out the email.

That evening, I prepared steak and was just slicing tomatoes for the salad when it happened.

Kill him…kill him…kill him…

I cried out and tried to drop the knife, but it stuck fast to my fingers. I couldn't release it. I no longer had control of my right hand.

Greg rushed to my side. If only he hadn't.

"Alex, whatever's the—" He never completed his question. His eyes widened and his mouth dropped open. Disbelief was the last expression I saw on his face.

I felt detached from mind and body, as if I was watching from a great distance. I saw him clutch his chest and fall back. I watched the spreading pool of blood stain his white shirt. I heard the thump and felt the vibration as he fell to the floor, while the knife dripped blood. It clattered onto the tiles as I regained control of my hand. I dropped to my knees.

I heard a long, drawn-out wail and realized it came from me. I stroked his face, and his sightless eyes stared upwards. I felt his neck and then, frantically, his wrist, but I knew there would be no pulse.

A shadow moved in the corner of the room. Margarita. And she was smiling.

I lunged at her amorphous shape. "Satisfied now, you bitch?" But I knew she wasn't. This was what she wanted all along and she would continue to use me to get her kicks for as long as I lived. A picture of Duncan swam into my head. He would be next and I would be powerless to stop it.

She'd won. In saving Grace Devine, I had lost myself. If only the girl's spirit hadn't entangled itself in my life. If only…

I stayed there, on the kitchen floor, all night, mourning my husband, sobbing out my grief, until no more tears would flow.

By dawn I had made up my mind. I wrapped Greg's body in a blanket and made my way upstairs, where I changed into a smart skirt and matching jacket, white blouse and black flat shoes. At eight-fifteen, with make up on and hair brushed, I looked like any other professional woman on her way to work.

On my way, I paused to make an anonymous call from a phone box to the emergency services. I had to ensure Greg was properly cared for.

Now I am here, on the platform, and the train is approaching. Will I have the courage to do what must be done?

May God forgive me and have mercy on my soul.

About the Author

Following a varied career in sales, advertising and career guidance, Catherine Cavendish is now the full-time author of a number of paranormal, ghostly and Gothic horror novels and novellas.

Her novels include: *The Stones of Landane, Those Who Dwell in Mordenhyrst Hall, The After-Death of Caroline Rand, Nemesis of the Gods* trilogy: *Wrath of the Ancients, Waking the Ancients,* and *Damned by the Ancients, Dark Observation, In Darkness, Shadows Breathe, The Garden of Bewitchment. The Haunting of Henderson Close, The Devil's Serenade, The Pendle Curse* and *Saving Grace Devine.*

The Crow Witch and Other Conjurings is a collection of her previously published and brand new short stories.

Her novellas include: *The Darkest Veil, Linden Manor, Cold Revenge, Miss Abigail's Room, The Demons of Cambian Street, Dark Avenging Angel, The Devil Inside Her,* and *The Second Wife.*

She lives by the sea in Southport, England with her long-suffering husband, and a black cat called Serafina who has never forgotten that her species used to be worshipped in ancient Egypt. She sees no reason why that practice should not continue.

You can connect with Cat here:

Website: catherinecavendish.com/
Facebook: facebook.com/CatherineCavendishWriter
X (formerly Twitter): twitter.com/Cat_Cavendish
Instagram: instagram.com/catcavendish/
Tik Tok: catcavendish
Bluesky @catcavendish.bsky.social

Curious about other Crossroad Press books? Stop by our website:
http://crossroadpress.com
We offer quality writing
in digital, audio, and print formats.

Subscribe to our newsletter on the website homepage and receive a
free eBook.